A FRESH KILL

ERYN SCOTT

Kristopherson Press

For the crafters, quilters, knitters, painters, DIYers, calligraphers, artists, and anyone else who creates beautiful things with their hands. You make the world a cuter place.

Hadley James's twin brother placed a hand on her shoulder as they stared at the **sold** placard stuck to the realtor's white yard sign.

"You sure about this?" Paul asked.

"I kinda have to be." Hadley sighed. "It's a done deal."

He shot her a worried look.

She chuckled. "Don't worry. I'm ready and I'm sure. I wouldn't have put it up for sale if I hadn't been sure."

"But you don't even have another place yet. Where are you going to live if you need more than the thirty days for closing?"

Hadley blinked. "Well, I kinda thought I could crash with you for a bit." She shrugged.

Paul bent his knees and then straightened them as he squinted up at the cornflower-blue summer sky.

As twins, Hadley and Paul had always been able to read each other, seemingly of one mind at times. At that moment, Hadley regretted knowing what her brother was thinking. That knee bend—not to mention how he wouldn't meet her gaze—was classic Paul avoidance behavior.

He paused just a heartbeat too long. "Uh, sure. Of course you can crash with me."

The offer came too late though. Hadley knew him too well for him to get away with even the tiniest fib. He didn't want her to stay with him? The possibility hit her in the gut as palpably as if one of his knees had landed there.

Hadley's mind raced. He'd offered to have her live with him just a few months before when her divorce had finalized, and she wasn't sure how she would feel living in the house she and Tyler had purchased together and had lived five years of their relationship in.

And because Paul could read Hadley equally as well, he must've realized—once he met her eyes—that she was taken aback by his answer.

He put a hand on her arm. "Not because … well, I was thinking of you. I mean, you don't want to move in with your smelly, bachelor brother." He grimaced, but she got the distinct impression he was trying to smile. "It's too bad Mom and Dad's place has renters or you could stay there."

Their parents were currently spending time in Oregon with their grandmother. After Hadley and Paul's grandfather passed away in January, their parents had taken time off work to go help. Losing her husband of sixty years couldn't have been easy, and they wanted to be there to help her adjust. But a month or so after they'd arrived, they realized that the house needed a lot more work than Gran could handle on her own, and she needed to come live with them. They'd only just started the process of fixing up the house in order to sell it, so it could still be months before they were back.

Seeing Hadley still wasn't okay, Paul reassured her again. "Of course you're welcome to stay with me. Anytime."

Lie. That's a lie, Hadley thought, pursing her lips into a thin line.

Though she could tell he was lying—plain as day—what Hadley didn't know was why. Checking her watch, she shook her head. Whatever Paul's deal was, she didn't have time to figure it out now.

"I've gotta run." She hoped she was able to keep the tightness from her voice.

Paul nodded. "Right, market day."

"And it's a big one." Hadley raised her eyebrows.

"Interloper Day?" Paul asked. "Already?"

Dipping her head once, Hadley kicked at a rock sitting near the toe of her sandal. "Yup, he'll be there today."

"That came up fast. It felt like this apocalyptic thing everyone talked about, but might not even happen."

"I know." Hadley shook her head.

Leo Morton, Stoneybrook's florist, had coined the term *interloper* in reference to Charlie Lloyd, the florist from Cascade Ridge. A twenty-minute drive was not all that separated Stoneybrook from the larger city up in the foothills of the Cascade Mountains. The only two pieces in the Grande County puzzle, they'd been in competition for as long as anyone could remember.

Stoneybrook citizens often talked about the people of Cascade Ridge as stuck up corporate pawns who measured their lawns. And Cascade Ridge spat equally harsh retorts back, calling the Stoneybrookians hicks who were stuck in the last century. The people of Cascade Ridge had a running joke that Stoneybrook's awnings were proof the town was stuck in the nineteen fifties. Each store had one, a different color matched with the white stripes for every new storefront.

For all of the heated words, Stoneybrook residents

knew people from Cascade Ridge were just jealous. At a quarter of Cascade Ridge's size, they were still the favored tourist destination in the valley because of their cute, locally owned and sourced shops. It wasn't just Main Street that brought people from all over the state. Often more of the draw was their famous year-round farmers market, something which had always been 100 percent Stoneybrook's.

Until that Saturday, when Charlie Lloyd was set to open his own floral booth and make local history as the first nonresident to sell wares at the market.

Sure, they had their outliers. Christine, who owned the valley's distillery, lived more than twenty minutes outside of downtown. Regardless of the distance, her business was still called Stoneybrook Spirits and she identified as a local. But Charlie would be the first real outsider they'd had.

He'd applied for the booth permit months before, but it had taken the local town council meeting after meeting to come to a decision on the matter. And while it was quite split, the vote had finally come down in favor of the interloper, citing the fact that if the town wanted to grow its tourism, one of the fastest ways to do that would be to open up their market to new, yet still *relatively local* vendors.

Leo Morton had not agreed, especially since he and Charlie had been butting heads in the floral sales space for decades.

"Well, you'd better get to it, then," Paul said to Hadley. "Don't want to miss any of the drama."

Hadley scoffed. "Right. You know, you should come too, on standby. It's only a matter of time before one of the florists strangles the other." She plucked the tan material of her brother's deputy sheriff uniform.

He shook his head. "I think I'll pass. I'm trying to stay

out of the line of fire." Paul pushed his shoulder back, wincing a little.

He'd been shot while investigating a murder case just a couple months earlier, and even though the bullet hadn't hit any major organs or arteries, it had clipped and fractured his collarbone. While the wound had healed, it had been a long process as it wasn't in a location where they could put a cast on the break.

Hadley dipped her head and patted him on his good shoulder. "Understandable."

"Want a ride into town?" he asked, motioning to the back of his truck.

"No, thanks. I've been eating too many of Mickie's scones." She patted her stomach. "I could use the exercise."

Paul waved goodbye as Hadley wheeled her bike from where it was leaning against her fence. She pulled her helmet on, tucking her long, almost-black hair into the helmet so it wouldn't fly around too much. Throwing a leg over, she took one more moment to look back at her now-former house as Paul pulled away.

Her heart ached, almost more than it had the day she'd signed her divorce papers. It wasn't as if she had been happy that day—far from it, actually—but between his frequent *business* trips and distant manner, Tyler had been gone long before she'd found out about his affair. Maybe seeing the house go was so hard because she couldn't even remember the happy, naïve young couple they'd been when they'd been standing out front all of those years ago, taking pictures in front of a similar sold sign. Or maybe it was tough because it meant she was finally letting go of what could have been.

A tear gathered in the corner of one eye, and she swiped it away. "Jeez, Hadley. It's not like you have to move out today." She shook her head as she scolded herself for getting so sentimental.

Paul's mention of their parents' house was another part of it. She missed them. And as nice as it would've been to be able to move in their house during her time in between residences, she mostly just wanted them here with her at such a crucial time in her life. Sure she was in her thirties now, but her parents were two of her best friends and their guidance was always appreciated. Taking a deep breath, she reminded herself how much they were helping Gran and that they would be home soon.

Kicking off, Hadley pointed her bike toward town.

Downtown Stoneybrook was about a five-minute bike ride from Hadley's home. And on a glorious summer day like today, she loved tipping her head back and breathing in the fresh mountain air of her hometown. The mighty Cascade River was a mere ghost, hidden behind a line of trees on this road, and Hadley could only hear the great rumble and rush of it. But she felt it too, as did anyone who'd grown up along its banks.

After the quiet of her backroads ride, the bustle of town hit her like a happy surprise party; people she knew waved as she rode through town toward the lavender-and-white striped awning sitting over Pretty Jam Good's canning head-quarters. Checking both ways, Hadley took the turn into the alley behind her building at a bit of a faster lick, knowing she'd spent more time than she should have chatting with Paul, and reminiscing about the sold sign.

Suzanne Till, Hadley's best friend, wasn't waiting at her back door, so she knew she couldn't be too late. Propping her bike up against the building, she pulled off her helmet and then fished out her keys. After unlocking the back door, the familiar, tart scent of her jam kitchen hit her like a welcome home. She couldn't help the smile that curled across her lips; she loved her business and felt like pinching herself whenever she thought about this being hers.

Knowing life sometimes got in the way on Saturday mornings, Hadley had gotten in the habit of packing up everything for the market on Friday before she left for the day. So even though she'd cut it a little close that morning, all she needed to do was load her boxes into the van and wait for Suze.

Boxes filled with glass jars of jam weren't light, so after moving a few loads into her affectionately named, Jam Van, she swiped at her sweaty forehead, then checked her watch.

"I can feel your *hurry up, Suze* vibes from down the street, you know," Suzanne said as she walked down the small alleyway.

Hadley raised her hands. "Sorry," she said. "I'm just a little anxious to see how this all goes down. At this point, we're going to be the last ones there, and I don't want to miss any florist fistfights."

Suze's eyes widened. "Omigosh, I know! I almost couldn't sleep last night I was so worried about how it'll go."

She loaded her box of art prints into the van while Hadley locked up the jam kitchen. Then, seat belts clicked on, they were ready to go.

"I do feel for Leo," Hadley said as she pulled the van onto Main Street. "I can't imagine if a person—especially one from out of town—started competing with me and selling jam."

Suze nodded. "Yeah, but flowers are in high demand at this time of year; there's plenty of customers for two florists. I think Leo's mostly sour because it's Charlie. Those two have been mortal enemies for years."

"Well, after Wedding Gate last year, I don't blame him. That was so low of Charlie."

"Speak of the devil," Suze muttered, gaze locked on Charlie's Bloom van parked sideways in the Fenton Park lot. The shiny, white van boasted **The Freshest Flowers Around** with its colorful decal.

Hadley eased her van in next to his, shaking her head. It was an unspoken rule that the vendors would park head in, even though many of them would've liked to pull in sideways for easier access to shimmy carts up to their sliding doors. They'd tried it one summer and parking had been a nightmare for everyone, especially customers.

Charlie was not only parked sideways across two spots, but the front of his van was facing away from her so it was in the shade of a large oak tree, Hadley's preferred spot.

That's what she got for showing up last. Taking a deep breath, she put a smile on her face. "We'll have to tell him about the parking agreement."

"Definitely." Suze grimaced as she slipped from the passenger side of the Jam Van and scooted around the back of Charlie's in the small amount of space left.

Unpacking the van onto two carts, the women pulled their supplies out onto the field and began setting up among the other booths.

On a normal Saturday, the vendors would wave and chat while they set up. But that morning, an uncomfortable hush had settled over the park, like all of those foggy fall days in the valley when clouds hang low and spit rain. Normally, people would've been focused on setting up their booths, but today all eyes were on Charlie's booth.

Hadley blinked.

Correction: the place where Charlie's booth *should've* been, but was still empty.

"Where is he?" she asked, looking to Suze, who also appeared confused.

They glanced back at the parking lot, hidden from the main market space by a small grassy knoll.

"That *was* his van, right?" Suze asked.

Hadley nodded.

She took a step toward Potholder Penny, the woman who made potholders—and only potholders—in the next booth over.

"Charlie hasn't been here to set up yet?" Hadley asked.

Penny shook her head. "Hazel thinks he must've chickened out. Good riddance, I say."

The words "no show" and "thank goodness" hung off the other vendors' lips.

"But he *is* here. He did show." Hadley refocused on Penny. "We just parked next to his flower van."

Penny's sour face wrinkled in confusion.

Hadley turned back to Suze, who'd already begun setting up her booth. "Hey, I'm going to run back," she said. "I forgot something in the van." She called the words over her shoulder as she walked over the grassy expanse back to the parking lot.

As the rows of vendor cars and vans came into view, Hadley felt a lump form in her throat. Charlie's van was definitely in the lot, so where was Charlie? She used a hand to block the sun from her eyes as she scanned for the forty-something man and his curly mop of hair.

Nothing.

Then she noticed something odd: a shock of red fabric showing through the window of his van. Hadley closed the distance between her and the van in half the usual time.

"Charlie?" Hadley called, heading straight for the driver's side door.

Her feet stopped moving—along with her heart—as she got close enough to see the red fabric was the short sleeve of a T-shirt.

Charlie was sitting in the passenger seat of his van, his head lolled forward, curly hair blocking his face.

Panic rose in Hadley, up into her throat, making it impossible to speak or call out. Instead, she gripped the door handle and pulled it open. Hadley jumped back as a handful of bees flew out of the van, barely missing her.

She swallowed the lump of worry in her throat, noticing the three large, swollen sting marks on his bare arms as she reached forward to check his pulse.

Nothing.

She staggered back, her wild eyes settling on the van's decal. **The Freshest Flowers Around**. Heat gathered in her throat. Fresh was right. Charlie's body was still warm. Reaching back to check her pockets, Hadley fumbled as she grabbed for her phone.

Paul picked up on the first ring.

"Looks like you're going to have to come to the market whether you want to or not. Charlie Lloyd is dead."

2

"Bees flew out when I opened the door," Hadley explained to Paul when he and the other Stoneybrook deputy sheriff, Kevin, arrived in the parking lot minutes later.

They'd found her sitting on the curb, trying in vain to rub the goosebumps from her arms, but she was beginning to feel better now her brother was there.

She rubbed her right hand up and down her jeans as she talked; there was something sticky on her fingers she couldn't seem to get off.

"Looks like he must've been allergic." Paul furrowed his black eyebrows as he studied Charlie's body.

Voice full of false hope, Hadley said, "Maybe there were bees on the flowers when he loaded everything into the van this morning. His van says they're the freshest flowers around."

The James twins looked in the back of the van at the buckets full of freshly cut bouquets.

"But they left him alone on the twenty-minute drive

down here from Cascade Ridge, waiting until he parked to sting?" Paul asked, skeptical.

Hadley glanced over her shoulder as Suze crested the small hill from where the market was still setting up. Her face darkened and she picked up her pace.

"I got worried when you took so long." She grimaced, glancing from the flower van to Paul and back to Hadley. "This doesn't look good."

"Sorry." Hadley sighed. "I should've texted you. I think I was in shock."

She filled Suze in on what she'd found, pointing to the crime scene and Charlie's still-warm body.

"Poor guy," Suze said in an exhale as she took in the scene. "What killed him?"

Kevin, who was examining the body, looked over his shoulder. "I'll have to wait until Doctor Hall gets here, but from the way he's swollen, it appears to be anaphylaxis. He must've been allergic to these stings he's got on his arms."

The three friends shook their heads and turned their attention to their shoes. Hadley felt awful for the man.

"Anything else you noticed?" Paul asked Hadley. "I think we're going to have to shut down the market for today. I want to question everyone while this scene is still fresh."

Hadley nodded in agreement. "He was here when Suze and I pulled up, but parked the way he is, I couldn't see into the driver's window until I came around to this side. We figured he was already setting up. But then Penny told us no one had seen him yet, so I came to check." Hadley squinted as she thought. "Then there were the bees and …" She rolled the tips of her fingers together, still feeling a tackiness there. "And my fingers are sticky."

Hadley walked around to inspect the driver's side door handle, knowing she'd used her right hand to open it. A sticky film coated a few areas of the metallic silver handle, matte in the morning sunshine.

"We'll have that tested to see what it is." Paul nodded to Kevin who went to his cruiser to grab whatever he'd need to take a sample.

"So you think it wasn't an accident?" Suze asked in a whisper.

Paul shrugged. "I don't know. At this point it's just highly suspicious." He rubbed the back of his hand against his bearded chin. "Kev, hold this down for a minute."

When the other deputy confirmed he would, they walked across the grassy park to break the news to the vendors.

§

"D ead?" Penny cried, covering her mouth with her hand.

The crowd of vendors gasped as they squeezed closer, some people looking confused, like they didn't hear correctly. The market hadn't opened yet, so he'd sent Suze to the entrance off Main Street to turn away any potential customers.

"I'm going to need to talk to anyone who saw him this morning." Paul's raised voice carried across the small crowd.

Murmurs wove in and out of the group, but no one spoke up until Hazel Smith yelled out, "That's just it. No one did."

Paul shook his head. "All of you vendors coming to set up, and no one saw him but Hadley and Suzanne?"

They blinked back at Paul with confused, scared expressions.

All except Hazel Smith, who pointed at Leo. "If

someone killed that man, it had to be him! He's been going on all morning about how he would love to get rid of the interloper for daring to encroach on Stoneybrook businesses."

Everyone's gaze swiveled to the local florist who scratched at the back of his arm.

"I—you can't think …" Leo stammered, backing up, hands out in defense.

Louise Stanton, owner of the local knitting shop, placed a hand on her hip. "What else are we supposed to think, Leo? You hated the man and then he shows up dead the same day he comes to compete with you?"

Murmurs of agreement sounded around the group. The two women were usually the only ones who were brash enough to say what everyone was thinking. It wasn't normal for the townspeople to do anything but support each other, but they were staying on the cautious side since one of their own had decided to off an old rival a few months earlier.

"We've been in competition for years. And sure, I didn't want him here, but I wouldn't kill him to stop him." Leo's eyes moved around to the faces of the other vendors as if trying to find one person to support him. "Louise, you agreed with me that we shouldn't let Cascade Ridge infiltrate our market," he pleaded.

Louise leveled an icy stare at Leo. "There's a difference between being upset by it and taking someone's life."

"Enough." Paul's deep voice cut through the argument. "Anyone with information will come through me. No more yelling accusations across a throng of people."

The vendors nodded, some stiffening at the firmness in Paul's tone.

"We're closing the market today. You may pack up, but

do not leave until you check with Kevin or myself. Clear?" Paul asked.

The vendors agreed and headed back to their booths.

As a group, the two-dozen faces of the vendors all seemed to meld together, but Hadley watched as they split up, keeping an eye out for any odd behavior. And even though she agreed with Louise that it didn't look good for Leo at that point, she hated to think the kind florist could've done something like this.

From the way the vendors looked over their shoulders and whispered, it was tough to discern any other suspicious behavior. Everyone was acting weird.

Until she spotted Barry Guthrie crouching behind his honey booth.

Hadley narrowed her eyes. Honey. Bees.

Barry's wild white hair was especially disheveled that morning. The harried man ran a hand through it and then picked up a box to fill with his stock. His gaze shifted as he began packing up his jars of golden honey. His hands shook as they placed each new glass back into the box. He swiped at his fingers with a handkerchief as if trying to wipe off something.

Immediately, Hadley's mind fought the idea Barry had anything to do with this. He was a sweet old man whose gentle soul calmed the people around him just as well as it did the buzzing bees living in his many hives. In fact, just last month, she'd seen the man break down and cry when three of his hives had been killed by a mysterious disease.

That wasn't a man who hurt or killed people.

But as much as she fought against the idea, Hadley felt more and more sure Barry was hiding something as he shook and startled at any noise.

Hadley bit her lip while she made her way back to her

cart. She hadn't even had the chance to unpack, so she didn't have anything to do at the moment. She definitely wasn't feeling ready to take her things back to her van, so near Charlie's body.

Suze had managed to unpack most of her art before coming to look for Hadley, and since she was helping turn away customers at the front gate, Hadley began to load her items onto the cart for her. After finishing and placing the boxes and folding table onto Suze's cart, she glanced over at Penny's booth where the older woman was just laying her last few potholders into big plastic bins.

Scanning the nearby tables, Hadley realized Josie still had quite a few pieces of pottery to wrap and pack, so she headed in that direction.

"Can I help you?" Hadley asked the potter.

Josie tucked back a lock of frizzy, red hair that had escaped her low braid. "Thanks, Had. It's going to take me forever by myself." She motioned to the crinkled, old newspaper she used to pack her creations from her studio and into customer's bags.

Hadley grabbed a large porcelain bowl with a wildflower design carved and painted onto it, and began wrapping the newspaper around it.

Josie was friends with Hadley's mother since they both worked at the local high school. And even though they worked in different departments—pottery and history were about as far from each other in the building as they were in study—they had always been the best of friends.

"This is just awful, isn't it?" Josie clicked her tongue as she shook her head.

Hadley nodded. "I know. You don't really think Leo had anything to do with it, do you?"

Josie paused, her fingers curling around a black-and-white plate with gold leaf flowers on it. "I can't say. I would hope he didn't, but I also know good people who've been pulled down by jealousy."

They packed in silence for a while before Hadley got up the courage to do some digging about Barry.

Licking her lips, she said, "Barry's acting pretty weird." She kept her voice low, even though when she glanced around, it was obvious they weren't the only ones making conjectures. Almost everyone else was having similar whispered conversations.

"He hasn't been himself since he lost those colonies last month." Josie sighed.

"I know," Hadley replied, wrapping a small cream pitcher and tucking it into a box. "He took it really hard. There wasn't anything he could've done for them, though." She packed away another bowl and then started to work on an assortment of mugs.

She startled as she realized Josie had moved closer, an intensity burning behind her brown eyes. "Didn't you hear?"

"No." Hadley held her breath.

"It *was* preventable. He figured out the bees died from a pesticide someone used on their flowers, not a disease."

Gasping, Hadley said, "But Leo uses natural pest deterrents in his garden." She knew that for a fact because she used to help him when she was in high school, and contemplating a degree in botany. "Fenton Farms is also organic."

Josie raised her brows suggestively. "But Leo and the Fentons aren't the only ones growing flowers around here, are they?"

Hadley pulled in a deep breath. "True." While she knew Stoneybrook had committed to using natural pest deterrents in gardens, that was all based on the honor system since it would be too hard to police. She packed up the last of Josie's mugs and closed the box.

"Barry's a sensitive guy," Josie said, closing up her last box too. "I'm sure it'll take him a while to get over the loss."

Nodding, Hadley focused on stacking Josie's crates onto her cart. She waved goodbye and then wandered back to her own cart, feeling lost. Paul and Kevin were talking near the edge of the market, their heads ducked together in confidence.

Suze walked up behind her. "Thanks for packing up for me." She hooked her arm through Hadley's and rested her head on her shoulder. "This day is the worst."

"Yeah, we should get out of here as soon as we can."

Suze nodded. "Sure, but I need to talk to Paul real quick. I think I may have seen something suspicious while waiting at the entrance to the park." She stood up straight.

Hadley wrinkled her brows in question.

"There was some lady parked the wrong way on Main Street wearing dark glasses and driving a fancy car. She was watching the parking lot, and when I approached her, she peeled out, took off."

3

After telling Paul about the mysterious woman she'd seen, Suze helped Hadley pull their carts back to the Jam Van.

Charlie's van was taped off, making it almost impossible to load their stuff. Terry, a local kid who helped out the sheriff's department from time to time, watched them from his post looking over the crime scene.

The women finally managed to unload the cart and were ready to take off when Hadley noticed one of her business cards had fallen out from her stack and slid under the tire of her van. She bent to retrieve it.

Crouching down like she was, something metallic glinting in the sunlight caught her attention under Charlie's van. It was right under the front end of the car, but would've been hidden to anyone who was standing.

"Terry, there's something over there." Hadley stood and walked around to the front of the van.

The young man frowned and unfolded his arms, following her and putting a hand out to hold her back.

"I'm not going to touch it." She put her hands up. "I just

want to show you where it is." Kneeling, she pointed to the small plastic case.

From a closer angle, she recognized it as a lipstick in a pink, plastic case with a silver, metallic band around the middle.

"Hmm … I'll let the deputies know, but I don't think I should touch anything either," Terry said, leaning down next to her.

"Right." Hadley agreed, though she was a little disappointed she couldn't read the brand or color name from where she was. "You've got it from here." She stood, wiping her hands on her jeans.

Suze was already buckled into the van, and she peered at Hadley through the window.

"I'm so confused," Hadley said, groaning as she climbed in the driver's seat and started up the van.

"Because of what Terry was just showing you?" Suze asked, waving to the kid as they pulled away.

"Of what I showed him." She described the lipstick as she drove down Main Street. "Why would Charlie have a tube of lipstick near his van?"

"It could've already been there this morning," Suze suggested.

Hadley pulled the van into the alley behind the jam kitchen and shook her head. "They've been running that community cleanup each Saturday morning since spring, remember? There hasn't been a speck of trash in the park or the lot before a market since they started." She clicked the ignition off and sighed.

"Oh right." Suze nodded. "So maybe we're looking for a woman with sticky hands and a vendetta against florists."

"I sure hope so, because the alternative seems to be poor

Leo, and I can't bear the thought he could've killed someone. Him *or* Barry."

"What does Barry have to do with this?"

"He was acting weird." Hadley waved a dismissive hand toward her friend. "But it was probably because he's sad bees were involved."

"Yeah, he *does* get emotional about bees." Suze shrugged.

"What did Paul say about suspicious, fancy-car lady?" Hadley asked, tapping her fingertips along the steering wheel.

"Asked for the make and model of the car, plus the plates."

"Which were?"

"Black, shiny SUV, but I didn't see the number on the plates." Suze shrugged.

Hadley waved her off. "I can't blame you. I don't know that I would've done any better at getting a description."

"But she was a lady. Ladies use lipstick." Suze held up a finger as if she were Sherlock Holmes himself.

Chuckling, Hadley opened the door and slid out of the front seat, then began lifting boxes. "Well, we'll just have to keep our eyes open for a fancy lady from out of town who wears lipstick. That won't be difficult or anything."

"Right." Suze's mouth twisted into a frown as she grabbed her art from the back. "Whatcha doing today since we have the day off?"

Setting down the box she'd picked up, Hadley said, "I should do more packing."

"I still can't believe your house sold so quickly."

"I know, though I shouldn't be surprised. Tara warned me that she was interested," Hadley said. "Though, it's going to be a little weird having my ex-sister-in-law living in my old house."

"A little weird?" Suze cocked an eyebrow. "That's a whole lotta weird, if you ask me." She stood and stretched, turning for the door. "I'm off. Going to take advantage of my time and finish up a painting Thea Clark commissioned."

"Hey, Suze?" Hadley's question stopped her friend just as she was about to leave.

"Yeah?"

"If I can't find a place by the time I have to move out, would I be able to stay with you for a bit?" Hadley held her breath, remembering the weirdness with Paul.

"Of course," Suze said, her face relaxing after having bunched up at Hadley's serious tone.

Hadley's shoulders sank down from where they'd been, tense and practically up to her ears. "Oh good. Thank you." She shook her head. "I asked Paul earlier, and he acted all strange and seemed like he didn't want me to. I mean, he offered months ago when Tyler and I split, but now it's like he's taking that back. So what's changed in those months? I don't understand."

Hadley had looked down during her vent session, but when she glanced up, the smile had slipped from Suze's features. She chewed on her bottom lip.

"Isn't that weird?" Hadley asked.

"Yeah. Super weird." Suze sighed and waved. "Well, I'm off! See you around." Tipping her head back in a goodbye since her hands were full holding on to her box of art, Suze headed down the alley toward her storefront three doors down.

Speaking of super weird, Hadley thought, *that interaction was not normal either. What's up with my friends?*

If it had been a decade earlier, she would've wondered if the two of them were hooking up behind her back—or maybe *hoped* was a better description. There wasn't anything better than thinking of her brother and her best friend being a couple. But she'd quickly realized that Paul and Suze were no more inclined to start a relationship than she and Hal from the country mini-mart. She shrugged. Maybe they were planning a secret birthday present for her or something, though that was a few months away still.

Unable to answer the questions floating through her mind, she entered the kitchen and got all of the stock from the day put away. Then she loaded some empty boxes into the van and decided to drive back home, not looking forward to figuring out how to ride her bike while carrying a bunch of cardboard.

Ansel, her small black-and-white cat named after the photographer Ansel Adams, greeted her when she got home. He serpentined around her feet, brushing up against her legs as she set down the flattened boxes and hung up her keys.

"Hey, buddy." Hadley picked him up, feeling her shoulders settle for the first time since she'd found Charlie's body that morning.

The gentle sound of Ansel's purring and the way he bumped his head into hers affectionately made her feel more at home than any house ever could.

"It's been quite the day," she told him. Then she went on to explain the morning's events.

Since she'd gotten the cat a few months earlier, taking over his care when his owner had been killed, Hadley often found it helpful to talk things through with the cat when she had a lot on her mind. Of course he couldn't talk back—or understand anything she was saying—but it helped her sort things out, often leading her to an answer when she couldn't find it any other way.

As she finished her story about Charlie and the odd assortment of clues so far, Hadley frowned, realizing that talking it through only made her more confused.

Setting the cat down, she said, "Oh well, Paul's on the case." While the thought was encouraging—her brother was a great deputy—she couldn't help but worry a little about his safety. Another murder investigation only reminded her of the last one when he'd been shot. She didn't know what she would do if she lost her brother. Discomfort tightened her shoulders. Hadley smiled and pushed away the thought, glancing back at Ansel.

"Besides, you and I have our own worries. We've got a month to find a new home, or we're going to be living out of the jam kitchen."

Ansel meowed as if in agreement.

Heading into the kitchen, Hadley began putting together some lunch. Then she settled onto the couch with a plate of food, a glass of iced tea, and her laptop. Ansel jumped up, settling on the back of the couch right by her shoulder. He liked to hang his feet over the edge, playing with her hair or occasionally clawing her arm and then acting surprised when she scolded him.

Hadley took a bite of her lunch and pulled up a real estate site. "Let's see what's out there."

The site must've remembered her last visit because her location was already preloaded and it brought up a list of Stoneybrook properties. Hadley hadn't gotten any farther than this screen the last time she'd logged in, so there weren't any other specifications loaded other than the zip code. That meant anything available in the area showed up on her screen.

She leaned closer to the screen, unable to believe her eyes as she looked at the newest listing.

She sucked in a surprised breath. "Leo's flower shop?"

While the man was younger than her parents by about ten years, he'd owned the store as long as she could remember. Hadley recalled how angry he'd been about Charlie coming to sell at the market. Maybe it was borne from more than just frustration with their long-standing feud. Was it possible last year's drama over the series of three wedding gigs Charlie stole from Leo—known around town as Wedding Gate—had done damage to more than just Leo's ego?

Hadley decided not to worry much more about Leo until she could talk with him about it. She stopped by every Monday when she went in to pick up her weekly order. Though the fact she hadn't heard anything about him selling before now meant he probably wasn't keen on talking about it. In a town as small as Stoneybrook, no one listed their house without everyone in town already knowing. So much so, Hadley often wondered why any of them used these realty sites in the first place.

Now she realized the sites' appeal over talking with people around town. The locals' information about available houses also came with a barrage of questions and judgments. She couldn't handle hearing any more opinions. Certain houses were just too big for a single woman. Was she sure she wanted to buy something before settling down with another man? Just remembering the ordeal made her wrinkle her nose.

She'd contacted Deborah Sandstrom, Stoneybrook's sole realtor, last week but every time the woman began asking her questions about what she wanted in a house, she found it difficult to decide on what she wanted next.

Did she want something already built or land to build on? Turnkey or fixer-upper? Large plot or close to town?

She and Tyler had been together since high school, so she'd always had him to help her with these big decisions. And, if she was being honest with herself, Tyler had been the one in their relationship to have the intense opinions. When Hadley looked back on their time together, she acknowledged that she'd been a fairly passive participant in their marriage.

She sat up. "I suppose now's as good a time as any to figure out what I want."

Clicking on the price-range box on the realty site's search engine, she began entering her preferences.

"At least an acre," she said aloud, clicking the box on her screen. "I'd like to be close to town, sure, but peace and quiet is worth more to me than being able to walk downtown."

Ansel stretched, and one of his paws landed on her shoulder. "I'll take that as an agreement." She smiled. She'd made one decision at least. That wasn't so hard. On to the next one.

She took away the option for plots of land, realizing that even though she might want to build a house someday, right now she needed to focus on growing Pretty Jam Good. That led her to the last check, which was *turnkey*. Hadley wasn't afraid of putting in some sweat equity, but it was all going into her business at that point.

Minutes later, with some paw-specific input from Ansel, Hadley had a good list going.

"At least two bathrooms, an acre or more. I want to be close to the river if I can, and I'd prefer three bedrooms but will work with two if I have to." She read it aloud, then nodded. "I think we can work with that."

Finger hovering over her keyboard, she took a breath and then hit enter, waiting for the results.

Forty-nine houses came up in the valley, but only seven were in Stoneybrook.

Well, it doesn't sound like I'm welcome at Paul's if I do end up homeless, and I'm still not sure about Suze, so I'd better get searching. She sighed and pulled out her phone.

"Hi, Deborah. It's Hadley James. Yeah, I think I'm ready to start house hunting."

4

Hadley found several houses online, and on Sunday afternoon, she waited outside her house for Deborah to pick her up to go look at some of them.

The realtor drove a flashy, white SUV, one you could spot anywhere in town parked among the farm trucks and backroads cars. Deborah always said she needed to have something nice to drive her clients around in, and Hadley supposed that made sense.

She didn't like to admit it, but there was a slight wobble of uncertainty still about this whole house-buying business. Hadley would've normally asked Paul or Suze to come with her, but Paul was busy figuring out who could've killed Charlie, and Suze had apologized but said she was busy when Hadley had asked her yesterday via text message.

The crunching sound of tires on her gravel road brought her back to reality. She closed her eyes and took a deep breath to calm her nerves. Opening her eyes, she stifled a laugh at the garishly fabulous sight of Deborah waving from the driver's seat. The woman's hair was bigger and blonder than a teased-out pageant queen; her makeup looked like it would curl like too much paint if someone ran a fingernail over her cheek, and she wore more bling than most rappers. Hadley also knew from experience Deborah's perfume was potent enough to smell at least two hundred feet away, and being confined in a car with her would most likely lead to a terrible headache at best and asphyxiation at worst.

Pulling open the door, Hadley climbed in, gulping one last lungful of fresh air before closing it behind her. With the soft thunk of the door into place came two sensory assaults. First, the dreaded perfume, which smelled like potpourri and baby powder had an evil love child. The second assault came when she noticed another person sitting in the back seat. Hadley jumped at the sight of him.

"Hey, Had." Luke Fenton's familiar voice felt like a punch to Hadley's already somewhat tender gut.

There were half a dozen reasons Luke had such an effect on her, but only three that were important, or at least that's what she told herself. First, they'd grown up together and had been good friends until high school when he decided he was too good for Hadley and Stoneybrook. Second, since he moved back to town from Seattle a few months ago, it seemed his main mission in life was to pull Hadley back into childish fighting with him, and—oh, yeah … third—he was her ex-husband's best friend.

"What's he doing here?" Hadley asked Deborah, jabbing a thumb toward the back seat even though she already knew. Deborah was infamous for trying to set up clients by taking them out house hunting together.

Luke clutched his chest and feigned pulling out an invisible arrow at her question, her tone, or both.

Deborah smiled her big, flashy realtor smile. "Well, both of you just happened to want to go house hunting today. Isn't it the cutest?"

Hadley felt strongly that no, it wasn't. She pressed her lips together. This had Deborah Setup written all over it.

That was the trouble living in a small town like Stoney-brook—people knew every aspect of each other's lives. Ironically, they often ignored the most important aspects—like how she and Luke had butted heads for the better part of a decade and barely tolerated each other—in order to push an agenda they believed in.

"Oh, don't worry, dear." Deborah patted her arm and then put the gearshift into drive, pulling away from Hadley's house. "Your lists of wants couldn't be more different. The two of you won't be competing for houses, I promise."

"Well, that's no surprise," Hadley muttered, glancing back at Luke.

He winked at her. She stifled a groan and buckled herself in, sealing her fate instead of jumping out of the moving vehicle like she sorta wanted to.

"We're going to one of Haddy's places first." Deborah hummed a nondescript song that kinda reminded Hadley of "Pop! Goes the Weasel."

She cringed—because of the humming and the nick-name. Hadley hated being called Haddy almost as much as she hated being called babe. The latter nickname had been coined by one of her classmates in high school when Paul had begun to grow his signature dark beard. Between the facial hair and his sheer size, people started to call him Paul Bunyan, after the mythical lumberjack. Hadley and Paul had always been close—built-in best friends, their mother called them—so it wasn't soon after Paul's nickname someone decided to be clever and call Hadley, Babe the Blue Ox, like Bunyan's sidekick. As someone who had always had to watch her weight—and often watched weight gather around her hips if she didn't take precautions or spend hours in the gym—Hadley didn't appreciate the moniker. Not in the least.

Just like she didn't appreciate having Luke Fenton foisted upon her without warning.

Deborah, seemingly unaware of the uncomfortable situation she'd put Hadley in, kept talking, filling them in on the house they were heading toward.

"It's got two and a half bathrooms," she said, pausing as she thought of the other characteristics.

"Oh, two and a half? Hmm … I want three." Luke shook his head.

Hadley fought the urge to glare at the man. Acknowledging his comment would only make him happy.

"There are two bedrooms, which I know is on the low end for you." Deborah tipped her head to one side.

"Two? I mean, where will your guests sleep? Hads, come on." Luke tsked. "You never want to put yourself in a situation where you're choosing between your guests' comfort and a home office."

This time, she did turn around, shooting him her best incredulous look. She knew Luke had grown up in a tiny farmhouse, and that kind of shallow talk was just his way of getting under her skin.

Deborah, missing the flat note to his sarcastic statement, wrinkled her heavily made-up forehead and turned her attention to Hadley. "He *does* have a point. Do you want to skip this one?"

"No, please. I would like to see it. My friends and family all live in town, so I don't have any guests who need a place to stay anyway." Hadley kept her eyes on the road as Deborah nodded and took the next turn down Huckleberry Lane, a small gravel road near the west edge of town.

Darn, Hadley thought to herself. *Maybe I spoke too soon.*

Despite the cute name, Huckleberry Lane had to be her least favorite area of Stoneybrook. It had neither a view of the river nor the surrounding mountains, but instead was surrounded by looming evergreens. And while she loved trees as much as the next Pacific Northwesterner, she was rightfully worried about the possibility of limbs or whole trees falling on her investment.

And that was all she could think of as they toured the cute little cabin. Luke refrained from adding any commentary, thankfully, instead just following the women and watching Hadley as she took in each new room.

Luke always told her he could read her like a book. Annoyingly, he was right much of the time. As the trio walked out of the house, Hadley schooled her features to hide the fact that—cute as it was—the house was a definite no.

"What do you think?" Deborah asked.

Before Hadley had a chance to open her mouth, Luke spoke up.

"This house is not going to work."

But instead of following up that statement by bringing up the lack of bedrooms again, Luke said, "She needs to be able to look out a window and see the mountains each morning and watch the sun set behind them in the evening. And when she walks outside, this woman needs to hear the rushing river as loudly as her own heartbeat. If either of those things are missing, I'm convinced her soul will shrivel up and die." He turned toward her and winked. "And we can't have that, now."

Even though the tone Luke had used was playful and teasing, she found his comment kind of sweet, as well as spot-on.

He cleared his throat. "Plus, the low number of bedrooms, of course."

Deborah glanced over as if checking to see if what he'd said matched with how Hadley felt. She nodded before looking down to hide the smile pulling across her face.

The great mountain views were her favorite thing about her current house. It just held too many memories of Tyler for her to stay any longer. She needed to move past that chapter in her life.

They all climbed back into the SUV, and Hadley felt her shoulders settle a little more, no longer feeling irritated at Luke's presence in the back seat.

"All right, Debbie. My turn next, right?" Luke asked.

Hadley shook her head. Well, not *as* irritated.

They toured a large four-bedroom house sitting right on the bank of the river for Luke and then a cute three-bedroom ranch with lots of character and three-hundred-sixty-degree mountain views from where it sat in the middle of the valley, for Hadley. Another practically palatial home got the thumbs-down from Luke when he noticed it didn't have a garage.

Tired of listening to the man nitpick beautiful houses when she could only afford half of what he could began to grate on her, so Hadley headed outside for some fresh air. She kicked at the pine needles blanketing the hard earth on the high bank of the river, wrapping her arms around her middle. A wonderful cool breeze whipped up off the water and twirled its fingers through her hair, some of which had fallen from her ponytail and framed her face. She swiped the toe of her sandal in the dirt to make a mouth and then made two short lines for eyes. Two dusty boots stopped next to her smiley face.

"Deb's just locking up." Luke shrugged, then focused on

her pine-needle-and-dirt design. "I remember you used to make these wherever you went. One time Paul and I found you and Suze on Jefferson Island just by following your sand smileys."

Hadley's lips tugged into a reluctant smirk "Better luck next time?" she asked.

Luke dipped his chin. "Yeah, there's just something missing. I'm sure I'll know what it is once I see it. But don't worry, I promise I will not be present during your next trip. I honestly didn't know she was making us look together until she picked me up."

Hadley sucked in a lungful of the river air, hating to admit the day hadn't been quite as terrible as she'd imagined it. "Good luck. When Deborah decides on a match, she's like a dragon with gold."

Luke laughed. "Right you are."

Glancing up at him, she said, "Hey, you know about pesticides, right?"

Tipping his head and lifting his eyebrows at her, Luke scoffed.

Hadley put up her hands. "Okay, okay. Sorry. Your move to Seattle must've made me forget, farm boy." Her expression turned serious as she remembered her question. "I heard about Barry's bee colonies being poisoned by pesticides. What kind could've done that?"

Luke's jaw clenched tight. "There are certain combinations of fungicides and pesticides that wreak havoc on colonies. I don't even know all that much about it, just enough to know I'm happy we're an organic farm."

"But aren't all of the farms in Stoneybrook organic?"

While Fenton Farms was by far the largest venture, there were many small outfits who made a living as well.

Luke nodded. "And Leo's garden along with the nursery out on River Road are too."

"As are the individual homes. The town council passed a measure three years ago which outlawed people from using pesticides in their yards."

"I heard about that," Luke said. "Of course, it doesn't include Cascade Ridge, but Barry's bees wouldn't travel so far. Their range is a few miles at most."

It was almost as if Luke anticipated where her thought process was going. Even though he hadn't been present at the market that Saturday, she knew he would've heard exactly what happened.

"Oh. I see." Well, that changed her theory. Charlie couldn't have impacted Barry's bees from that far away. Hadley chipped away at her nail polish as she thought.

"So sorry," Deborah said, scurrying over to them. "That darn lockbox gave me one heck of a time. Ready to go?"

Hadley and Luke followed Deborah back to her car. Hadley dragged with her the realization that this process may take longer than she had before she needed to be out of her house.

❧ 5 ❧

Monday morning, Hadley biked to the jam kitchen. Before she unlocked the place, she walked three buildings down to pick up her flower order for the week. Stoneybrook was free of any large chain stores and chock-full of local businesses. They looked out for each other, promoted wherever they could. After all, a dollar spent in Stoneybrook was a dollar toward a stronger town.

In addition to sourcing her labels from Suze's design company and using local produce in her jams, Hadley liked to set up a large vase of flowers from Valley Wildflowers in each of the three picture windows on the street side of her jam kitchen.

She stopped in front of the violet-and-white striped awning hanging above the Valley Wildflowers sign.

A bundle of silver bells tied to the front door announced Hadley's entrance as she pulled it open and stepped inside. As always, the first thing to hit her was the smell of the store. From the light, sweet smell of the fresh greenery to the more intense perfume of the flower petals, she felt herself sucking in a deep breath through her nose in an effort to appreciate each unique scent.

And that wasn't where the delights stopped. The place was a visual anti-depressant. Each color, so intense and perfect, worked together to create a palette that made her smile.

Some people had worried when Leo had first announced his plans to stop outsourcing and carry local, in-season wild-flowers about a decade earlier. They figured the limitation would alienate people looking at roses for winter weddings or any other out-of-season wish. The result, however, was that the town was surprised by the vast array of local species and learned to embrace whatever was in season at the moment.

The front door jangled shut behind Hadley and someone blew their nose from behind a fern in the back right of the shop.

"Oh, hello!" Jessie, Leo's daughter poked her head out from behind the large green fronds, blowing her nose into a tissue with one hand and holding up the other in a *just a minute* gesture. After she'd finished wiping her red nose, she smiled. "Sorry about that. My allergies are crazy bad today."

Hadley's forehead wrinkled as she took in the poor young woman. She did seem miserable. Normally, Jessie glowed. From her long, blond hair to her flawless skin, the young woman was the picture of beauty. Today, her eyes were rimmed with red, and the chapped skin under her nose led Hadley to believe that tissue hadn't been her first and wouldn't be her last.

"Are you allergic to the flowers?" Hadley asked.

Jessie exhaled, her youthful face adopting a beaten down, tired expression. "Quite a few of them, I'm afraid."

"I had no idea." Hadley shook her head. She didn't remember ever having seen the girl so affected in all the years she'd known her. "That must be terrible."

Jessie shrugged. "I usually take medication for it, but I've been trying some natural remedies lately, you know, to be less dependent on pharmaceuticals. Unfortunately, nothing I've tried so far is working."

Sniffing once more and then tossing the tissue into a garbage can behind the register, Jessie straightened her shoulders and said, "Dad left your order all ready. I'll go grab it."

Before Hadley could say anything else, the girl disappeared through a door Hadley knew led to the cold flower storage in the back. She returned a few moments later, clutching two vases while the other was held tight between her arm and torso.

Hadley's eyes lit up as they roamed over the mix of white lilies, magenta hollyhocks, blue columbine, pink lewisia, and three bright yellow sunflowers. Rich green salal and a few sage-colored grasses completed the look, pulling all of the other colors together.

Jessie set them onto the counter. "He did such a great job this week, didn't he?" She beamed as she surveyed the arrangements.

"He always does. It's my favorite part of Monday morning." Hadley smiled. She loved how Leo would go through each flower, explaining what it was and some fun fact about it. After months of picking up vases, Hadley felt as if she'd gotten a full course on local flora. She was even able to identify most of the plants in her own garden thanks to Leo's lessons.

Speaking of Leo, Hadley wondered where the man was. She loved talking to Jessie—the nineteen-year-old was usually away at college, and it was great to see her home during the summer to help her father with his shop—but Hadley had been hoping to see her father, especially after seeing his shop listed on that realty site.

"Where *is* your dad? I was hoping to talk with him." She didn't mention why she wanted to talk with him, unsure if Jessie was aware of her dad's financial troubles.

Jessie chewed on her bottom lip for a second before answering. "He isn't feeling well. I told him I would run the show today."

Nodding, Hadley said, "I suppose that makes sense, considering ..."

"Right." Jessie picked a stray leaf from the counter and flicked it into a compost bin. "I hear you were the one who found him. What happened?" She glanced up, eagerness gleaming behind her eyes.

Hadley was sure Jessie knew exactly what had happened on Saturday. There wasn't a person in the lower valley who wouldn't have heard at least four different accounts of Charlie's death. However, Hadley also knew it was a common Stoneybrook practice for citizens to ask questions to which they already knew the answers in order to maintain the illusion the town didn't run solely on gossip. Even the town's younger generation was well versed in the expectation, as was evident from Jessie's question.

"It was awful," Hadley said. "If you don't mind, I'd rather not relive it."

Jessie shot her a small smile. "I understand. Sorry to bring it up. I guess I'm still shocked."

"Everyone is."

At that, Jessie scoffed. "Not everyone, it seems," she mumbled.

Hadley tipped her head to one side. "What?"

Jessie blinked up at her as if she'd forgotten she was there. "Oh, there are just a few people who seem to think Dad had something to do with Charlie's death. They said they weren't surprised Charlie showed up dead with the way Dad's been threatening him."

"Yeah …" Hadley pulled in a deep breath.

"Dad wouldn't bend a flower petal on purpose, let alone do anything to hurt a person." Jessie's voice rose and her tone wavered.

Hadley nodded. "I know. We all know that, Jess. It's just the threats he was making toward Charlie make him look super suspicious now. He's got a good alibi for that morning. Surely enough people saw him at the market, at his booth. The police will clear his name in no time."

"Thanks for your support."

"Are you sure you're good?" Hadley asked again. "What happened to Charlie is awful. It would make sense to be sad about it," she said, wondering briefly if the girl was masking her tears as allergies.

Shaking her head vehemently, she answered, "I'm not saying Charlie deserved to die, but I definitely won't be shedding a tear for him. He's been awful to my dad for years, and the guy's a *complete* creep. Well, he was …"

Hadley hadn't encountered Charlie too many times, but in the times she had, the man made her uncomfortable, touching her without asking and calling her pet names when they'd just met.

Jessie, obviously done with their conversation, pushed the vases closer to her on the counter. "Do you need any help carrying these?"

Hadley wrapped an arm around one vase and then grabbed the other two with her hands. "Nope. I'm a pro by now."

The color returned to Jessie's face as she smiled. "Have a great day."

As Hadley exited the store, she felt a little tickle in *her* nose now that her face was surrounded by blooms. It must've just been the power of suggestion, though, because she'd never had an allergic reaction to the plants before, and while she knew it was possible to develop them as one got older, she doubted it was anything more than sympathy allergies.

The thought reminded her of Charlie's bee stings. As an adult, he had to have been aware of his allergy, if it was bad enough that three bee stings could bring on such an intense reaction. Someone who worked in an industry where bee stings were a given couldn't *not* know they were deathly allergic to the insects, right? If he hadn't known, it was possible his death had been a freak accident, the poor guy being in the wrong place at the wrong time.

If he *did* know he was allergic, though … Jessie's comment about allergies and the different medications she'd tried came to mind. Assuming Charlie knew he was allergic and he had still decided to work as a florist, he must've had something precautionary like an EpiPen just in case of an emergency. And if that was true, why hadn't he used it that morning? Anaphylaxis would've taken a few minutes, at least. Plenty of time to reach for an Epinephrine pen. But she hadn't seen anything of the sort near him inside his flower van. Of course, she hadn't noticed much beyond his body.

Hadley pondered that as she walked down the street back toward the jam kitchen.

"You're a walking hazard with those." The gruff voice stopped her, and she turned to see her brother standing, arms crossed, as he shot her a playful smirk. He stepped forward. "Here, let me take a few before you walk right into the road."

Smiling, Hadley handed over two of the three vases. Paul followed her as she rounded the corner into the back alley and unlocked the jam kitchen's back door. It was usually such a chore each Monday to try to locate her key in her pocket and unlock the door with all of those vases in hand, so Paul's help was appreciated.

"So what's got you all spacey this morning?" Paul asked, setting the two arrangements he held on the tables in the front windows. He walked over to her and took the last vase, setting it on the last table before returning his attention to her.

"What?" she asked, arranging the flowers even though they were still perfect. "I'm not spacey."

Paul chuckled. "Right. You regularly zigzag across the whole sidewalk making pedestrians run out of your way. Sorry. I must be wrong."

Hadley pulled an apron over her head and focused on tying it behind her back to avoid the fact that Paul had a point.

"Plus, you've almost no more nail polish left, and I swear you just painted those the other day."

Oh, great. I must've been picking at it while I was talking with Jessie. She curled her fingers in even though he'd already noticed the lack of light-purple polish.

She sighed. "Okay, sorry. I was thinking about Charlie and Leo."

Paul raised an eyebrow. "How so?"

Hadley told him about seeing the flower shop for sale, and explained her wonderings about Charlie's allergy preparedness.

"We've been looking into it. Apparently Charlie did have

a prescription for an Epinephrine pen, but we haven't found anything of the sort in the van." Paul rubbed a hand over his dark beard.

"Any luck finding Suze's mystery woman or figuring out how she's involved in this whole thing?"

Paul shook his head. "Kevin and I are going up to Cascade Ridge this morning to go through Charlie's home with Sheriff McKay to see if there are any clues there."

Hadley felt her eyebrows lift as if of their own accord.

"Nope," Paul said, leveling her with a serious stare. "Don't you get that interested look. You are not coming with. We've got this under control, Had."

She knew Paul getting shot had shaken him just as much as it had her. Paul seemed intent on keeping her away from any further investigation, saying he couldn't forgive himself if something happened to her. But what Hadley couldn't forget was the fact that she'd been the one to save his life; that his gunshot wound would've likely been fatal if she hadn't disobeyed him and gotten involved. So even though she knew he wasn't going to be happy with her, she couldn't help but investigate.

Paul interrupted when she opened her mouth in protest.

"I'd better get going." He patted her shoulder and headed out through the front door.

Once Paul was out of sight, Hadley slipped her phone from her purse and texted Suzanne.

Wanna go up to Cascade Ridge for reasons which definitely don't include digging around at Bloom while Paul's busy with the rest of the deputies at Charlie's house?

Suze texted right back.

Pick you up in ten. Get coffee.

Hadley smiled and grabbed her wallet.

❦ 6 ❦

H adley stood outside the jam kitchen ten minutes later, two lattes clutched in her hands as she watched Main Street for Suze's powder-blue mini. She jumped, almost spilling the coffees when a black sedan pulled into one of the slanted spots in front of her and honked.

Bending down to get a look at the driver, she was startled to find Suze behind the wheel.

"Hey!" Hadley said as she opened the passenger door and climbed in.

"Sorry for honking," Suze replied. "I don't know how to work the windows in this fancy thing." She glanced cluelessly at the complicated dashboard of the fancy car.

"I didn't know you were getting a new car."

"Oh," Suze chuckled. "This isn't mine. I swapped with Hazel for the day. Figured Paul would spot my car instantly. Cascade Ridge is a big place, but a powder-blue car is a powder-blue car."

"Good point." Hadley nodded, glad Suze had caught on to the clandestine nature of their mission.

"Get yourself buckled. Kevin and Paul were walking out

to the cruiser when I was driving past town hall." Suze checked the rearview mirror. "If we want to maximize our searching time, we'd better be on their tail."

Hadley complied. "Thanks for understanding," she said, glad her friend was on the same page.

If she'd told most people that she was worried about her big, burly brother, they would surely laugh in her face. But Suze knew Paul almost as well as Hadley; she understood he was much more sensitive than he let on and that his injury would have worse lasting emotional effects than physical. Plus, the three of them had always been better together than apart.

Hadley surveyed the car. "I didn't know Hazel had such a fancy ride."

Hazel Smith was Suze's longtime neighbor. She worked at the local pharmacy and was the head of the Stoneybrook Quilters Association. She was also the town's paramount gossip.

"She just got it. Said she's been saving up for it for years."

"And she's letting you drive it?" Hadley cocked an eyebrow at Suze.

Suze elbowed Hadley. "Cut it out, if you still want a ride. I'm an incredibly safe driver."

"I know you are, but I'm pretty sure the loan has more to do with Hazel thinking the world of you."

While both women had known Hazel since they were little, Suze always had a soft spot for the older woman and vice versa. Suze's grandma had lived in the house next to Hazel until she died a few years ago. They'd grown even closer when Suzanne had inherited her grandma's house.

"Well, who can blame her?" Suze joked. Then, without

much warning, she reversed and pulled out onto Main Street, following the deputy cruiser as it went by.

"We know how to get to Cascade Ridge." Hadley chuckled. "You don't have to follow them."

Suze shrugged. "It'll make the most of our time if we can get there as close to when they arrive at Charlie's as we can."

Hadley filled Suze in on the new developments in the case while she drove. They had to pay close attention, making sure they didn't get too close to Paul and Kevin; even in a different car it would still look suspicious. Hadley explained all about her chat with Jessie earlier and her thoughts about Charlie's unfortunate bee allergy.

"Poor Leo," Suze said as they drove up the winding road to Cascade Ridge. "I can't believe people think he could have done something like this. Barry either."

Hadley picked at her nail polish.

"Wait. You think it could be one of them?" Suze let out a small gasp.

"No. I don't know." Hadley shrugged. "I just don't want to let my feelings for people make me overlook the truth."

Suze took her eyes off the road for just a moment to look at Hadley. Short as it was, the glance was full of meaning, telling Hadley Suze understood why that was so important to her. Hadley had always prided herself on seeing the best in people, but last year she'd found out her husband of ten years—and high school sweetheart—had been cheating on her and had spent all of their savings. After that, Hadley vowed to not let people take advantage of her trust again, trying to become a shrewder judge of character.

"I understand," Suze said, smiling over at Hadley as the busy streets of Cascade Ridge came into view. "Okay, now where'd you go, Paul?" Suze scanned the roads for the green cruiser.

"There." Hadley pointed to the car taking a left about a mile ahead of them. "I think we're good to head to Bloom now."

Suze clicked on her blinker and drove toward one of the larger shopping centers. She took the next left onto one of the busier through roads in the city.

"If I remember correctly, Bloom is up in the next business complex." Hadley pointed ahead.

Unlike Valley Wildflowers' storefront—which featured a wood-carved sign made by Hadley's dad and hand-painted lettering on their window done by Suze herself—Bloom was in a fancy new building next to a Panera Bread and had a sign that looked like it cost more than half the businesses in Stoneybrook made in one quarter. They exited Hazel's car and made their way up to the shiny glass doors, shading their eyes with their hands as the midday sun reflected off the large windows.

"It's closed." Suze's voice was as flat.

Hadley sighed. "Of course it is. The owner just died. I can't believe I thought it would be open." She inwardly rolled her eyes at her mistake. Maybe Paul was right to keep her off the case. "I guess we came up here for nothing."

Suze nodded. "Bummer."

Dejected, they climbed back into Hazel's car. They rejoined traffic in silence, and Hadley stared at a big semi-truck rumbling along next to them on the two-lane highway that cut through Cascade Ridge. Semitrucks weren't something they saw often down in Stoneybrook, the town's infrastructure too small and its businesses in no need of such large deliveries. Hadley's heart felt like it'd been run over by the huge machine.

She sighed as Suze clicked on her blinker and pulled in behind the truck.

"Omigosh!"

The car screeched to a near stop. Then Suze flipped on her blinker and pulled into a block of two parallel-parking spots in front of a row of businesses. Hadley glanced at the street, then at Suze.

"It's her!"

"What?"

Suze pointed at a bench next to a bus stop about ten feet in front of them on the right. The bench featured one of those realtor ads that ran along the whole back rest. This one featured a woman with a sincere smile and smart, dark-brown hair worn in a bob. **Vivian Harris, Vanderberg Realty**, read the advertisement.

"That's the woman I saw parked in front of the market on Saturday, the one who sped away when I went to warn her about parking in the tow-away zone."

Hadley's eyes widened, realizing what this meant. "It's her?"

Suze put up her hands and smiled. "It's her!"

Both the women looked over at the bench and the picture of Vivian's face one more time.

"Technically *you're* in the market for a house." Suze cocked an eyebrow.

"Not in Cascade Ridge, though!" Hadley scoffed, offended she would even consider that an option.

Suze dipped her head from side to side. "Well, of course, but Vivian doesn't need to know that."

"Oh." Hadley's mouth formed a little circle. "Right." She began to nod the more and more the idea sank in. "Okay. We could do that. Do you think she'll recognize you, though?"

Letting out a scoff, Suze waved a hand at Hadley. "The woman peeled out so fast, I doubt she noticed anything about me."

Satisfied, Hadley found the realty office's address on her phone and Suze plugged it into the car's GPS. Excitement built in Hadley's stomach as the GPS began directing them toward Vivian, possibly toward some answers.

Vanderberg Realty was housed in a large, beautiful building that overlooked the valley from its perch at the southeast edge of the city. Hadley gaped at the office, having a hard time not comparing it to Deborah's tiny office in downtown Stoneybrook. She immediately felt awful for doing so. Vanderberg Realty was a national chain competing with the likes of Windermere, John L. Scott, and even Sotheby's. Hadley preferred the intimate setting and small-town charm to this fancy operation any day.

"This place is fancy." Suze let out a whistle then snapped at Hadley, pointing at the glove box. "Can you reach in there and grab me a hair stick from th—" Suze's face fell. "Oh darn. I forgot this isn't my car."

Suze's hair sticks were well known in Stoneybrook. Gathered from the riverbanks, Suze sanded and painted unique pieces of wood and kept them as single chopsticks to hold up her mass of brown curls whenever she got over-whelmed. From the unique patterns and colors to the way they only seemed to work in Suze's wild locks, those *hair sticks* were something Hadley had always associated with her best friend.

"Well." She shrugged. "I guess I'm going in full volume, then." Suze fluffed her curls, and they got out of the car.

Hadley sucked in a deep breath as they approached the building and headed inside. A whoosh of air wrapped around them, smelling of a recent remodel, all new carpet and just-dried paint. A chipper, lanky, young woman sat behind a sensible desk in the foyer. Hadley smiled back at her when she beamed up at them.

"Welcome. What can I do for you today?" she asked.

"We're here to see Vivian Harris," Hadley stepped forward, Suze right by her side. "I'm moving into town and would like to look at some properties."

The receptionist nodded. "Sure thing. Who can I tell her is asking?"

"Hadley James."

The girl picked up the phone. "Hey, Viv. When's your first appointment today?" The girl glanced up at Hadley, winking. "Oh, perfect. You have a couple women here who are moving to town and would love to talk with you if you don't mind starting a little early. Great." She put the phone down and said, "You're in luck; she has time to see you right now."

Hadley and Suze thanked the smiling girl and then stepped back to wait.

Before long, the clicking of heels echoed out from the tiled hallway. Vivian Harris stepped out into the foyer like she was stepping right out of her bench ad. Her hair looked camera ready, as did her gray skirt suit and wide grin.

Unlike Deborah—whose smile pushed the limits of dentistry, and whose makeup was thick enough for the stage —Vivian was put together in an understated way that made her all the more appealing.

"Hello," Vivian said, walking toward them with her hand outstretched. "Vivian Harris. Lovely to meet you."

"Hadley James." Hadley shook her hand, feeling quite self-conscious of her chipped nails as she got a look at Vivian's expertly manicured set. She stepped aside so Vivian could shake Suze's hand. "This is my friend, Suzanne Till."

Vivian greeted Suze and then held her arm out toward the hall she'd come out from. "Why don't we talk in my office?"

She led the way to the back corner of the building and ushered them into a room that took Hadley's breath away.

Okay, maybe not everything about Cascade Ridge is terrible, she thought to herself as she looked out the two large picture windows opening out to the North Cascades. While Hadley had spent her whole life staring up at these same mountains and could name each peak, this was a different view. She could even see the row of mountains beyond the valley.

"Wow, that's quite the view." Hadley exhaled for effect.

Vivian beamed as she took a seat behind her desk. She glanced out at the scenery like a proud mother looking at her child. "It's like my slogan says, 'Cascade Ridge is the best place to live. Hands down.' That wasn't an overstatement when I wrote it." Looking back to Hadley, she asked, "Where are you relocating from?"

Torn between the beauty outside the window and her irritation at yet another example of Cascade Ridge residents' belief that anywhere else—especially Stoneybrook— was terrible, Hadley took a moment to answer. She was tempted to lie to save herself from the frown she knew would come once she revealed she was from Stoneybrook, but she also couldn't think of a better way to get Vivian talking about Charlie, so …

"Stoneybrook." Hadley cringed, like someone waiting to be slapped.

But instead of launching into the usual diatribe against the small town to the south, Vivian's face went pale, and her open mouth clamped shut.

Feeling the awkwardness wrap around her throat like a

hand, Hadley swallowed. "But … I just got divorced, and I think I need to get out of there. You know, my ex's family lives there and it's a little awkward still. A fresh start would be good." Hadley stopped herself, realizing she was rambling to cover up her discomfort.

As if she'd stopped listening at the word "Stoneybrook," Vivian's eyes narrowed, and she turned her attention to Suze.

"You're from Stoneybrook? That's why you look so familiar. You were there on Saturday."

Suze gulped, glancing over at Hadley for a moment before turning back to Vivian.

"Uh, yeah …" Suze squeaked out the answer.

Maybe it was how the realtor's amiable disposition had changed to a decidedly less-friendly version of her, or it was the chill which seemed to settle over the room, but Hadley worried they'd made a huge mistake by coming there alone.

7

Vivian smoothed a *let's sell you this house* smile over her previously concerned face. "Stoneybrook is adorable." Her gaze shifted between Suze and Hadley. "I wanted to check out your famous farmers market, but I saw people being turned away. I guess it just wasn't my week."

"Sorry about that," Suze said.

"It's kind of terrible, actually," Hadley said, seeing her opening. "There was a death at the market." Hadley searched Vivian's face as she took in the news.

The woman gasped. "Oh no. That's terrible." Her hand flew up to cover her mouth.

Suze nodded. "It was awful."

"He was from Cascade Ridge, not Stoneybrook. Charlie Lloyd? He owns a floral shop up here, Bloom. Did you know him?"

Vivian blinked, then shook her head. "No, I'm sorry to say I didn't. There are a few florists in Cascade Ridge, and I can't say I know any of them on a first-name basis. But we're not like you small-towners; we don't know every one of our neighbors the way you folks do."

Hadley smiled to cover up how hard she was gritting her teeth.

"That stinks you didn't get to look around at all," Suze said, inserting herself into the conversation when she must've noticed Hadley was growing irritated.

Picking up a pen from her desk, Vivian clicked it open and then closed it again. "Yes, a shame. Well, enough about that. Adorable as it is, Stoneybrook is stuck in the past. We definitely need to get you out of there. What's your price range?"

Hadley quoted the same amount she'd shared with Deborah the other day. She and Tyler were splitting the sale of the house, so the equity they'd built up over the past five years wasn't much, but it would at least help her with a down payment.

Instead of smiling and nodding—as Deborah had—Vivian inhaled, long and slow. "The market up here is much more competitive, I fear. That added to the fact that our homes just trend higher because of the views and better location …" Vivian's forehead wrinkled, and she pulled out a pad of paper, jotting a few things down. "It'll be tough, but I can find you something, I'm sure." She smiled up at Hadley.

Fighting the urge to roll her eyes at such stereotypical Cascade Ridge behavior, Hadley matched the woman's grin. Thank goodness she didn't have to buy up here, pretending she was going to was hard enough.

"That would be great," she said around the fake smile.

"I could have some listings pulled for us to view by the end of the week. Does that work for you?" Vivian clicked on her computer and typed blindingly fast for a few seconds before she looked back up.

"Yes, that works." Hadley nodded.

Vivian stood. "Great. I'll give you a call. If you wouldn't mind leaving your number with my receptionist, she'll get in touch when I've got a firm date and time."

Agreeing she would, Hadley stood to leave, Suze following behind. And after stopping to give her phone number at the front desk, they scurried out into the parking lot. Hadley puffed up her cheeks and let her breath release slowly as they climbed into Hazel's car.

"Ugh. As if I could hate Cascade Ridge anymore than I already do." She sighed. "At least I won't have to see Vivian again. That story checks out. She must've just been there for the market."

Suze, who hadn't said much the whole meeting—uncharacteristically—pressed her lips together. "Sorry Had, but you're going to have to go back."

"What? Why?"

"While you two were talking, I was looking around her office. She has a file organizer behind her desk labeled 'Vendors,' and one of the files said, 'Charlie Lloyd - Bloom.'"

"That liar," Hadley snapped, slapping her hand down on her leg.

Calm, cool, and put together as Vivian appeared, Hadley would take the overdone Deborah, her setups, and her poisonous perfume any day over Vivian Harris.

"And if she lied about knowing Charlie, she could be lying about why she was in Stoneybrook the other day," Hadley said, calming.

People from Cascade Ridge always did this to her too. Knowing it wouldn't help to yell, she resorted to picking off the last bit of her purple nail polish.

"Hey, you're getting flakes all over Hazel's car. Knock it off." Suze swatted at her.

"Sorry. Okay, what do we do now?"

"You have to take your appointment with Vivian later this week. I'll come with you again, but we need to figure out a way to get her talking about Charlie. I want to know why she lied about knowing him and what she's trying to cover up."

"Fine. I'll call to set up an appointment, but let's get out of here. I'm missing home like crazy."

Suze agreed and pulled out of the realty parking lot. Traffic in Cascade Ridge was nothing compared to a city like Seattle, but for Hadley and Suze, having grown up in Stoneybrook—where there wasn't even one stoplight—the whole thing felt frazzling and frustrating. Despite the traffic, Suze navigated them back to the main highway through the city. The route took them past Bloom again, and Hadley stared at the building as it passed by her window.

"Is it just me, or does Bloom look open now?" she asked, noticing rows of lights on that hadn't been before.

Suze didn't even take her eyes off the road, instead just flipping on her blinker and pulling into the parking lot. After parking, she bobbed her head up and down to better see the store. "I think you're right."

Shrugging, they got out of the car.

When they entered, a young man stood behind the counter. He was tall and handsome, though a good ten years younger than Hadley and Suze. He had long, wavy, brown hair sitting just at his broad shoulders. He swiped it back out of his face as he smiled at them.

"Good afternoon, ladies. Welcome to Bloom."

"Hi," the women said simultaneously.

"Can I help you find anything in particular?"

Hadley pulled in a deep breath of the fragrant air as she looked around. The place was large enough to have eaten Valley Wildflowers whole and still have room to gobble up three other flower shops along with it. Not only did Hadley recognize some of the native flowers she was used to seeing in Leo's shop, but there were also the standard types she was sure they carried year-round.

Cookie cutter as it was, Hadley glanced at the arrangement the young man had been working on when they entered; it was gorgeous. He was an artist for sure. Suze appraised the piece as well, and from her raised eyebrows, Hadley could tell her artistic friend approved.

The young man cleared his throat, still waiting for an answer.

"Sorry, we're not usually this spacey. It's been a weird day." Hadley stepped closer to the counter.

The young man's face softened. "No worries. Just let me know if you need any help."

"Actually," Suze said. "This is our first time in the shop. Do you own it?"

Any kindness evident in the man's features hardened over. He shook his head. "I'm just the assistant manager. My boss owns the place … er—he did. Sorry, it's been a weird *couple* of days for me."

"That doesn't sound good." Hadley hadn't missed the anger that flared up when he talked about Charlie. She stepped closer to the young man so she could read his name tag.

"It's not. He died." Stuart shrugged. "I didn't open up this morning, but it didn't feel right. I didn't know what else to do, so I eventually came in to work like normal." He looked around the store nostalgically.

"I'm so sorry." Hadley locked eyes with him. "Does that mean you're out of a job?"

Again, Stuart shrugged. "I don't know." Then he huffed out a deprecating laugh. "I should know that, huh?"

Suze and Hadley smiled along with him.

"We had a few things in the works—a second store, some changes to this one. But ..." Stuart shook his head. "Now I don't know where any of that stands. I've worked here since I was sixteen. I don't know what I'll do now."

"Your boss's lawyer will be able to help you with all of it. I wouldn't worry about it now. I'm sure he thought about you." Hadley knew she was leading, but she kept on going. "If you've worked here that long, you and your boss must be like family."

Stuart barked out a humorless laugh. "That's a good one. No. That's the one clear thing in this whole situation."

Suze wrinkled her forehead. "If you two didn't get along, why did you continue to work here for so long then?"

Sighing, Stuart said, "He was a master manipulator. Each time I sounded like I was going to quit, he'd offer me a carrot and convince me to stay. Then things would get a little better for a bit. But after a few months, we'd be right back where we were."

Hadley chewed on the inside of her cheek as she thought. She knew Charlie wasn't a nice man, but it also sounded like Stuart was kind of silly for not leaving. Or, maybe Stuart wasn't telling the whole story.

She was about to ask if their business worked with Vanderberg Realty, and if so, in what capacity, when the shop door opened behind her, letting in a burst of air.

"Uh oh ..." Suze mumbled under her breath, jabbing at Hadley with her elbow.

Hadley turned to see what Suze was looking at and groaned. Paul loomed in the doorway, arms crossed in front of his chest and an eyebrow cocked in disapproval. Her stomach lurched; she was never going to hear the end of this.

8

Hadley turned back to a confused Stuart and pasted a fake grin on her face. "I'm so sorry. In an unexpected turn of events, we must go. Immediately." She grabbed on to Suze's forearm and tugged her toward the door.

"But we'll be back," Suze called back to him.

"Oh, no you won't," Paul grumbled, following the women out the door.

Out in the parking lot, Hadley turned to Paul. "What a weird coincidence. We were just looking into some flowers for … uh …"

"Price comparison," Suze said, coming to her rescue.

Hadley nodded, thanking her friend in her thoughts.

The hard creases on either side of Paul's mouth told Hadley he didn't buy it. "It doesn't matter if Valley Wildflowers started charging in gold coins, you'd never choose anything in Cascade Ridge over Stoneybrook. Cut the act, ladies. Just tell me what you were doing."

Knowing Paul would take the fact that they were worried about him about as well as a bull seeing red, Hadley's mind searched for alternatives.

"We had so much fun helping you on the last case, we thought we could be your Scooby gang," she blurted out.

"Scooby gang?" Paul cleared his throat.

"Yeah." Suze nodded. "You have to admit, we make a pretty good team." She pasted a big smile on her face.

Hadley did the same.

Paul narrowed one eye. "No offense, but this isn't a cartoon, and I'm a deputy, not a teenage boy with a goofy dog."

"Yeah, but you've said it before yourself; we can find things out that people won't always tell the police. Like how we discovered Stuart in there pretty much hated working for Charlie." Hadley curled her fingers into her palm to keep herself from pointing at the shop. Stuart might be watching.

"And we found the suspicious lady from the market on Saturday," Suze added, pursing her lips into a smug smile.

At that, Paul straightened a bit, and just a fraction of anger slid from his face. "Who is she?"

Suze said, "A local realtor named Vivian Harris. She works at Vanderberg Realty, and she lied to us, told us she didn't know Charlie even though she had a file which proved she'd used his company before."

"Got it. I'll go check her out. But I think it's time for you two to head back home."

Hadley and Suze adopted the same narrowed glare.

"We just gave you two really good clues, and you're going to send us away?" Suze asked.

Paul frowned. "I appreciate your help, but this isn't Stoneybrook. We can't get by on knowing people and hearing everything through the gossip mill."

"Everyone gossips, Paul, not just small towns." Hadley put a hand on her hip.

"Yes, but I'd feel much better if you two could focus on

our town. Talk with Leo, figure out why Barry was acting so weird. Please leave the questioning up here to me."

Hadley and Suze glanced at each other. Suze wet her lips, and Hadley pressed hers together in a thin line.

"Okay," Hadley said after a moment. "We'll go back." She put her hands up in surrender.

"Good luck," Suze called over her shoulder as they walked back to Hazel's car.

Once inside, they sat there in frustrated silence for a few seconds.

"I hate getting kicked off the case," Suze wrinkled her nose. "It makes me feel like a teenager all over again—so many rules and things we're not supposed to do."

Hadley held up her pointer finger. "But we didn't get kicked off the case. He just relegated us to local issues. That's not bad."

"True." She tipped her head to one side. "So does that mean you're not going to see Vivian again if she calls to set up an appointment?"

Hadley chewed on her bottom lip. "I'm not sure yet."

Suze smiled and then started the car. They tried to forget all about murders and victims and alibis as Suze drove them back to Stoneybrook. Returning home after venturing up to the bigger city for a few hours felt akin to wrapping herself up in a fluffy blanket and sinking into her couch, Ansel curling up by her side. Hadley sighed. Paul was right, this town was her wheelhouse, and she and Suze could get to the bottom of things here.

She waved goodbye when Suze dropped her off at the jam kitchen. Inside, Hadley puttered around for a few minutes. Already a few weeks ahead on her production, she checked her online orders and didn't see anything new.

She exhaled and looked around her kitchen.

Technically, she should be at home right now, packing up and getting ready for her inevitable move. Grabbing her purse, she cursed herself for being so on top of things in the jam business and headed home.

An hour after arriving at her house, she had managed to play with Ansel, organize her books based on spine color, and buy a new set of aprons online for her jam kitchen to replace her ratty, old ones. She stared at the empty boxes in her living room.

Just when she was about to get up, her phone rang, startling her but putting a smile on her face. Hadley grabbed at it. Maybe it was Paul with more information about the murder. Her heart beat in anticipation.

Deborah's name flashed on the screen.

Hadley pressed her lips forward. Not Paul, but not bad either. She answered it.

"Hey, Deborah."

"Hadley, honey. I know we just saw each other yesterday, but I felt so bad there wasn't anything you were drawn to, and I wanted to make it up to you. I found two places I think you'll just love. Are you free today at any point?"

"Right now is great, if that works for you."

There was a pause on the other end of the line. Deborah cleared her throat. "Uh, yeah. I'm just about to show someone else around and … well, from how you acted yesterday, I got the vibe you weren't into being stuck in the car with him."

Luke.

Hadley glanced around her house. It was either deal with Luke or stay here and be forced to pack up.

She sighed. "That's okay. I'm fine sharing you. You can come get me now."

From the squeal that followed, she was afraid she would

live to regret those words. If Deborah thought they would make a great couple before with no evidence whatsoever to support her theory, Hadley saying yes to spending more time with him would surely convince the matchmaking realtor they were meant to be.

"Oh great!" Deborah said. "I'm just about to head out the door."

Hadley paced around for a few minutes until Deborah's SUV pulled up in front of her house. Saying a quick goodbye to Ansel, Hadley pulled the door closed behind her and jogged up the driveway, climbing into the air-conditioned vehicle. Minutes later, she and Deborah pulled up in front of the tenant house Luke was living in on the edge of Fenton Farms.

Mouth hanging open a bit, Hadley scanned the secluded meadow surrounding the small house. She hadn't been back here for years; she'd forgotten how magical the place was. Tall grass swayed in the breeze sitting tucked up around the house, looking as soft and fluffy as if it were drifts of cream-colored snow. Stately pines surrounded the meadow, giving the place an enclosed feeling, like it just might be the only house in the world. Regardless of the trees, the house still had a great view of some of the larger peaks of the nearest mountains as they peeked up over the treetops.

Hadley sighed, peace washing over her. She rolled down her window, knowing she would hear the rushing of the wind through the grass layered with the louder sound of the river flowing just yards past the meadow. The smell of warm soil and pine needles flowed in through the open window as she focused on the house. It was the least remarkable thing on the property. It was small, outdated, and could use new siding, a new coat of paint, and a new roof … to start.

Luke exited through the front door, smiling as he spotted her through the open passenger window.

"Couldn't get enough of me yesterday?" He smirked as he slipped into the back seat.

Hadley turned around. "It's been an informative day. For example, I've learned my annoyance with you is not greater than my hatred for packing. So, yes, tease away. I'm immune to it today."

Luke chuckled, buckling himself in. "Where are we off to, Debs?"

The realtor stiffened at the nickname, but covered her distaste with a smile. "We have two houses, one for each of you." Before either of them could say anything, she added, "But don't worry. I think you'll love them."

The scenery around Stoneybrook often took Hadley's breath away, and she found it happening all over again as Deborah drove them around the backroads of the town. The A-frame Deborah showed Hadley first, however, did nothing to change her breathing. It was cute and close to the river, but there was nothing about it that wowed Hadley or made her feel a connection with the house or property.

"No worries. I'll keep searching," Deborah said as they climbed back into the vehicle, but her rigid posture revealed her downtrodden feelings.

Hadley, too, felt frustrated. At this rate, she would never find a place to live and would be forced to become a burden on Suze since Paul had acted weird about her moving in.

Dispirited, Hadley tried to focus on Luke's next house. They passed by Barry's farm, and Hadley scanned the dozen stacked boxes sitting in the field. Remembering the story about so many of his bees dying, Hadley pressed her hand against the glass and tried to think happy thoughts for the rest of them.

Just past Barry's farm, Deborah took a right and traveled down a dirt road, pulling to a stop before a gorgeous new construction house with an old construction feel. It had cedar siding and brilliant white trim, which accented its forest-green door.

"Okay." Luke got out and strutted around the property. "This is not half bad, Deb. Not half bad at all."

Hadley followed Luke and Deborah inside the house for the tour.

It was amazing. There were views of the mountains from most of the rooms, the river was right through the trees, and it seemed to have everything on Luke's list. This *had* to signal the end to his search. He couldn't possibly be so picky.

"I don't know." He shook his head. "I like it. Like—like it, like it. But do I love it?"

The indecisive shrug which followed rendered Hadley to all of twelve again and all she wanted to do was roll her eyes and let out a frustrated groan. Being an adult, she simply walked away.

She knew she was being childish, but after seeing Vivian's looks of pity that morning as she explained how much more everything was up in Cascade Ridge, looking at houses with someone who had loads more disposable income felt … well, annoying.

Hadley's wandering took her around back and she found herself in the landscaped backyard. It was the perfect mix of neighborhood and wilderness, a small radius around the back porch was cultivated while anything ten feet out was untamed forest. Following a footpath out to the edges of the property, Hadley walked toward the sound of the river. Maybe that would calm her down. But before she even reached the river, something to her right caught her eye.

She followed the shock of color in the otherwise green and brown forest, moving through what looked to be an animal path toward a small meadow. It probably used to be a meadow, but now was being used as a beautiful garden full of flowers. The tilled land and the fact they were growing in rows told Hadley these flowers had been planted on purpose, despite them all being native species to the area.

"Find a secret garden?" Luke asked as he stepped up behind her.

Hadley jumped, her hand moving to her chest as she let out a breath. "Maybe. It seems too far away from the house to be a part of the landscaping, but it's too deliberate; someone had to have planted all of this." Hadley walked forward and held the head of a beautiful sunflower in her palm.

"Not to mention someone's been here harvesting." Luke knit his brows together for a moment as he bent down to inspect the stem of a flower that had been freshly cut.

Hadley understood his need to inspect. What she didn't understand was when he leaned over and smelled the plant's leaves and then swept his thumb across the surface. As he stood, Luke rubbed the tips of his fingers together like she had the morning she'd found Charlie's body and had gotten the sticky substance on her skin.

"What?" she asked, taking a step closer to him.

"These flowers have been sprayed."

"With water?"

Luke shook his head. "Pesticides."

Hadley blinked. "Which means someone hasn't been following the rules."

"Looks like it." His blue eyes seemed to cloud over, like a summer day overtaken by a storm.

9

Minutes later, Hadley and Luke walked Deborah back to the secret garden they'd found behind the house. The second time approaching the hidden plot of land felt a lot less magical now that Hadley knew about the chemicals coating the leaves and petals.

"I know you probably don't have the property line memorized, but do you know if this garden is part of the property we were just looking at?" Luke ran a hand over his light-brown stubble.

Deborah bobbed her head. "I would say so. It's a ten-acre plot and this is only a few hundred feet from the house. It must be a part of it."

"Who owns this land right now?" Hadley asked.

Deborah fidgeted with the hem of her blouse. She glanced from Hadley to Luke. "It's ... well, Jack and Sarah Henley do."

Henley. The last name felt like a sucker punch to Hadley's gut. And from the way Luke's expression fell, he was equally affected by it. She shouldn't have been surprised. Her ex-husband's family was a Stoneybrook staple. They were everywhere around here. And Jack, Tyler's father, had a knack for real estate, flipping properties before anyone even knew he'd purchased them.

But while Luke and Hadley were both surprised to hear the last name, their shock was bred from different reasons. Whereas Hadley's came from the general dread which now encompassed anything having to do with her ex-family, Luke's came from the fact that he and Tyler had been best friends since childhood.

"The Henleys?" Luke's face was set like a block of concrete. Then he began to shake his head. "No. They're not farmers."

He was right. The Henleys, while having lived in the Cascade Valley for generations had always been into real estate and business. Tyler's mother and father owned the grocery store in town, his uncle ran the local ice cream shop, and his aunt kept a popular café. Tyler had gone to school for accounting. Not a one of them were farmers. And even if they had been, Hadley couldn't imagine any of them being the kind to treat their plants with town-banned pesticides.

Hadley may disagree with them about a lot of things— and half of them may still not be talking to her after the divorce—but she refused to believe the family she had been a part of would do something so terrible.

Deborah shrugged, missing the piece of information about the pesticides, and so, not understanding what was so bad about owning a garden. "I'm sorry, Luke. I thought you might be thrilled to take the place because of who owned it." Deborah leaned in close to ask, "Is there a reason you don't want to buy from the Henleys? Have you had a falling out?"

The question was so Stoneybrook, Hadley had to

suppress the urge to shake her head. She also knew the act of Deborah asking the question meant half the town already thought he did, regardless of Luke's answer.

"Not at all," Luke answered, then glanced over at Hadley for a quick second.

He was one of the few people in town who knew the actual reason Hadley had asked for a divorce from Tyler this year. When they'd first let their families know, Tyler had said they'd simply grown apart, omitting his infidelity. Hadley had been so shocked in the moment she hadn't contradicted him. Once she came to her senses, it seemed petty and unnecessary. After growing up in a small town, it was kind of nice to keep a secret.

It didn't hurt she was also incredibly embarrassed about having missed the signs. Regardless of the hurt she'd felt at being cheated on and the financial strain he'd placed on her with the cost of his extravagant affair, Tyler was also someone she'd known her entire life. She wasn't about to be the one to go around town telling everyone what had happened.

Luke cleared his throat and turned to look at Deborah. "I was just … uh, curious about who owned the place, that's all." Gesturing back toward the house, Luke motioned to get them to start moving.

The short walk was awkward, the unspoken things hanging between Luke and Hadley felt like a whole other person. They hadn't talked much about the affair, other than Luke apologizing for knowing toward the end and not knowing how to tell her.

She couldn't hold a grudge against him for keeping it from her, sure she wouldn't have been ready to hear it from him. In the end, the woman he'd been sleeping with, Christina, had contacted Hadley, hoping it might be the catalyst to Tyler leaving her for good as he'd been promising he would.

And even though it had been almost a year since she found out—and months since her divorce finalized—she still wasn't ready for people to know. She didn't want to deal with the sympathetic looks she would get for months after once they did know. A small part of her was still waiting for Tyler to be the one to tell everyone, a hope that became more of a dream once he'd decided to move to Seattle a few months ago.

"So what do you think?" Deborah asked as they got into the SUV and buckled up.

Luke's voice was tight in that way it got when he was lying. "I'm interested. There are a few things I would like to ask the Henleys myself, if you wouldn't mind."

Deborah smiled, missing the small intonations Hadley had caught. "Sure thing. You let me know how you'd like to proceed."

Pulling out onto the road, Deborah began to chat in length about paint colors and the mistakes people often make when pairing them, but Hadley couldn't focus on her words. Luke cleared his throat, and she glanced back at him.

His blue eyes narrowed as she met them, his lips pressed into a thin line. Suddenly, she was transported back in time to when they were younger, and it seemed like she could read his every thought, and he knew hers.

Hadley had always wondered if being a twin, how she and Paul had a bond regular people didn't, made her more susceptible to these telepathic-like connections. As it was she, Paul, Suze, and Luke had been inseparable growing up, and for a long time, it had felt like it wasn't just Paul whom Hadley could read.

She still felt like that with Suze. The woman could cock

an eyebrow or grunt, and Hadley knew exactly what she was thinking. They often texted each other at the same moment, seemingly on the same wavelength.

And even though she and Luke had grown apart in high school, he maintained he could still read her just as well. She couldn't read him like that anymore.

Except in that moment.

Just with one look, Hadley knew Luke wanted her to come with him to talk with the Henleys.

She shook her head. *Heck no!* She sent him a scowl, hoping her actions were subtle enough to escape Deborah's attention as she moved into the horrid mistakes people make with drapes.

When she looked back at Luke, he was holding up two fingers, almost like a peace sign. He curled them down twice, looking almost like he was using air quotes. Hadley knew otherwise. It was their secret, childhood sign for a double dog dare.

Seeing it again brought back so many silly memories that she couldn't help the laugh that burst out of her. Deborah caught it, but the woman was blindly entrenched in the world of home interiors and seemed to assume Hadley had found something she'd said about drapes hilarious and said, "It *is* funny! Isn't it?"

Hadley suppressed a grin and shot a glance back at Luke one more time. Rolling her eyes, she reluctantly nodded, telling him she accepted. After all, they'd taken an oath to only use the double-dog-dare gesture when completely necessary. She pretty much had to. And when Deborah dropped him off a few minutes later, Hadley knew the hand he held up in a wave was him telling her he'd come pick her up in five minutes.

For the remaining time in Deborah's car, Hadley tried to

focus on her words. They parted at Hadley's house, her slipping out of the passenger seat and waving to Deborah.

"I'm sorry the place didn't work out today, dear." Deborah's forehead wrinkled. "But we'll find you something, I promise."

Hadley waved a hand. "No worries. I've got time," she said, pushing down the feelings of worry that she definitely didn't.

Turning her back, Hadley headed toward her home, but she didn't go inside. Instead, she settled onto her lime-green love seat and waited for a moment until Luke's truck pulled up where Deborah's had just dropped her off.

He rolled down his window as she stood and walked over.

"You're a liar," he said, propping his arm on the door as he leaned out of the window.

Cocking an eyebrow, Hadley said, "I am?"

"A few months ago, you told me you couldn't read me. I'm sorry to break it to you, but you just did, Hads."

She laughed, climbing up into the passenger seat of the truck, feeling like she was back in high school. "It was some sort of time warp, I think. Once you brought out the dare it felt like we were thirteen again."

His lips pulled into a smirk that was so quintessentially Luke, Hadley felt her lungs pull tight with nostalgia.

"But you're right," Hadley added after Luke put the car in drive.

Luke glanced over at her, a question written in his knitted brow.

"You're getting easier to read again," she said. "You're coming back."

His eyes squinted up as he grinned. "I've been back for months, actually." He watched the road.

"You know what I mean."

He paused, then dipped his chin. "Yeah, I do." After a quiet moment, he said, "You are too, coming back."

Hadley cocked an eyebrow. "I'm not the one who left."

Luke's smile faded, his jaw muscles tightened in his cheek. "You did, Had. You weren't—" His voice cut out, and he shook his head. "I think a part of you knew … about Tyler … long before."

Hadley's heart ached as she realized he was right. She'd spent so many nights wondering how she'd missed the clues, asking why she hadn't noticed this or asked that. But there was a part of her that had always known she never fully had Tyler's heart or his attention.

Before either of them could say anything more, however, Luke pulled onto Main Street, and the time for talking about the past seemed to have done just that, passed. Pulling up near the orange-and-white striped awning of the Main Street entrance to the Henley Family Grocer.

While it was difficult to avoid the sole grocery store in town, Hadley had done her best to get everything she could at the farmers market and Hal's Food N Stuff minimart. In fact, over the last four months, she could count on one hand the number of times she'd entered the Henley Family Grocer.

The white tile floors reflected the florescent lights. Their sneakers squeaked as they walked inside. In all of her excitement about the case, Hadley didn't stop to think why Luke wanted her there with him until they were scanning the aisles for Mister or Missus Henley.

"Wait." Hadley pulled Luke to a stop in the cereal aisle. "Why am I here with you, again?"

Luke blinked. "To help me figure out why they've got a secret garden."

"Yeah, but they hate me. This isn't a good idea. I think you should talk to them alone."

Luke caught Hadley's flighty gaze with his. "Had, I'm counting on the fact that they hate you. You're part of the plan, babe. I want them flustered so they'll be less likely to lie. Don't worry, I'll get rid of you at the first dirty look."

A mixture of anger at his use of the nickname and worry about seeing the Henleys rendered her speechless, so Hadley nodded and followed Luke the rest of the way down the aisle. His eyes lit up and he came to an abrupt halt, moving back by the cereal to hide.

"Okay, Jack sighting. I'm going to start talking to him and then you come up after a minute. Say hello, try to start a conversation." There was a sparkle in Luke's eye as he recounted the plan.

"That's the dumbest plan ever." Hadley crossed her arms over her chest.

"It may be dumb, but it'll work." Luke winked, then touched his finger to the tip of her nose. "Trust me."

❦ 10 ❦

After Luke walked away, Hadley strained to hear from her hiding place by the bagged cereals. The plastic crinkled as she slid along the shelf farther toward the end of the aisle.

"Hey, Jack! How are you?" Luke did a great job of sounding pleasantly surprised.

A thump came next, which sounded like Luke slapping a hand onto the older man's back, or possibly enveloping him into a tight hug.

Just as Hadley was about to emerge from her hiding place, Luke said—louder than was necessary, which meant he wanted her to hear—"Sarah! You came out of nowhere. So good to see you."

Hadley pressed her eyes closed, tight. She hadn't run into Tyler's parents for months and still wasn't sure if she was ready. But she also wanted the information about the garden on their property, so if Luke thought her making things awkward would help that, it was worth a shot.

Opening her eyes and exhaling her worries, Hadley walked out from the cereal aisle and just about bumped straight into Luke's back. She hadn't realized how close he was standing.

"Sorry," she said, flailing to avoid running into him and stumbling off to the right. Once she found her balance, she sent a fake look of apology toward him. With one last deep breath, she steeled her courage and looked where the Henleys stood.

The cold, angry faces glaring at her weren't a surprise. Even the awkward way Jack cleared his throat wasn't enough to unnerve her. But when Sarah, someone whom she used to consider a mother, curled her lip and glared at Hadley like she was the human equivalent of freezers full of spoiled food, she began to doubt the plan.

"Oh, uh … hi there." She smiled, or maybe it was a cringe. "Hey, Luke." For some reason, in the moment, Hadley went with the whole *glad to have you back* routine. "How are you liking being back home?" she asked.

Luke's amused grin seemed completely real, unlike her forced questions. "It's great." Luke bobbed his head.

"Why do you want to know?" Sarah asked with a sneer. "Are you going to run him out of town too?"

Hadley balked. "Sarah, I—"

Luke settled a hand on her arm, turning to point her in the other direction. "Maybe you should … go." He winked at her, to let her know she'd done what he needed.

"Right." She sighed as she shot one last, sad look over at Sarah and Jack, then headed back down the cereal aisle, stopping when she was just out of sight so she could still hear.

"Have you heard from Tyler lately?" Sarah asked, her tone softening.

Hadley's spine stiffened, and she leaned closer to hear Luke's answer.

"Uh, yeah." Luke must've known she would still be listening in, because his voice was awkward and clipped. "Sounds like he's doing well."

"He calls us when he can, but he's so busy. I'm not complaining; it's just hard when we've been used to him living here in town." Without seeing her, Hadley knew Sarah was spinning the simple gold band on her right ring finger. She always did that when she was worried.

And even though Hadley knew she hadn't been the reason Tyler moved away—though having him live elsewhere was much easier for her, so she wasn't complaining—her heart still hurt for Sarah and the rest of the Henleys. If Hadley felt like she'd lost touch with the man she'd married, she couldn't begin to imagine how his family felt about this new, city-dwelling version of their favorite son, cousin, brother, etc.

"We're glad to have you back in town, though," Jack said.

"Thank you," Luke replied. "Actually, that's part of the reason I wanted to talk with you. Deborah showed me the property you two are selling out on Meadowvale, just past Barry's place, but I'm interested in the wildflower garden in the woods behind the house."

"Oh, that's not ours," Sarah said quickly. "I mean, we're renting it out to someone."

"But don't worry, we told him he could only use it until the place sold." Jack cleared his throat. "Not that it's an issue anymore."

"Why?" Luke asked.

"Well," Jack lowered his voice. "It was Charlie. He approached me after we denied him at that first town council meeting, asking if there was anything he could do to change our minds about letting him be a part of the market.

I told him he might have a better chance if he could claim his flowers were grown in town."

"And when did you find out he was using pesticides on the flowers?" Luke's voice was low, but Hadley could tell he was trying to keep his tone nonthreatening.

"What?" Sarah scoffed. "Luke, you know we wouldn't allow any—"

"After the bees died." Jack interrupted his wife.

"Jack?" She sounded incredulous. "I can't believe you kept that from me."

"By then the damage was already done. I promise I didn't know about it before then. I even went to apologize to Barry, offered to pay him for the damages to his colonies, but he would have none of it. All he wanted to know was who was responsible."

"And did you tell him?" Luke asked.

Nothing but silence followed. Frustrated and needing to know the answer to the question, Hadley leaned around the end-cap of the aisle to see what was happening. In her haste, Hadley knocked over the cardboard stand holding a new kind of granola. The bags went skidding across the bright, linoleum tiles, a few stopping at Luke's feet and one smacking into Sarah's sneaker.

The three of them glanced over at her and every expression on their faces made her want to die. The Henleys' because the accident only seemed to deepen their anger with her, and Luke's because his smirk told her it would be a long time before he let her forget this.

"I'm so, so sorry." She scrambled forward, righting the cardboard display. Gathering the bags in her arms, she attempted to reset them.

Luke helped her, grabbing the ones that had slid the farthest. After setting the last one upright, he wrapped an arm around Hadley's shoulders and said, "Good seeing you two, but I'm going to escort Miss James out of the store before she does any more damage."

She wanted to glare at him, but Hadley was too embarrassed to look up from the floor. She gave a sheepish wave and let Luke be her eyes as he rushed them down the aisles. A summer breeze cooled her hot cheeks as they walked outside.

"Well, that was terrible." She covered her face with her hands.

Luke chuckled. "It wasn't all bad."

Letting her hands drop, she finally met his gaze with a withering one of her own.

"What? We learned an important clue. Charlie was the one responsible for killing so many of Barry's bees. And Barry refused money, but wanted the name of the person who'd sprayed the pesticide? That sounds like a man out for revenge to me."

Hadley shook her head, turning back toward Luke's truck. "Barry's not one of our main suspects."

"He's not?" Luke's eyebrows lifted skeptically. "Pretty sure he should be. A man is killed with bees after he poisons a good portion of the colonies owned by an intense bee lover. Sounds like a Stephen King novel, sure, but it seems to check out to me."

They reached the truck and Luke unlocked it. Once they were inside, Hadley said, "Sweet, kind Barry? I don't buy it. Plus, we're looking into some woman up in Cascade Ridge. I think she's our killer."

"Wait, you're seriously not even considering Barry?" Luke turned to look at her instead of putting the key in the ignition. "And what about Leo? The man flat out threatened Charlie the day before he turned up dead, and he was furious about Charlie encroaching on his market space."

"Leo brings huge vases full of flowers to the hospital up in Cascade Ridge whenever he can. He regularly puts fresh flowers on every gravesite in the Stoneybrook Cemetery. He made the flowers for my wedding. I've known him my whole life." Hadley buckled herself in. "I refuse to believe he had anything to do with Charlie's death."

Luke's face hardened. "Just because you know and love these people doesn't mean anything, Had. Good people get angry too. Good people make mistakes and bad decisions. Don't be so naive to think you know everything about people just because you've known them for a long time."

The statement stung. Hadley knew she had the tendency to trust too blindly, but having Luke point it out felt so much worse, somehow. She covered up her pained expression with disregard.

As quick as she'd been to hide her emotions, the deep lines between Luke's eyebrows told her he'd still seen the effect of his words.

"I'm sorry." He shoved his key into the ignition and sighed. "That was a crappy thing to say, Had."

Hadley smiled over at him. "It's okay. I—you're right. I'll make sure to include Barry and Leo on my list of suspects. I'll let Paul know right away what we learned about the connection between Charlie and Barry's dead bees today."

Returning her not-so-convincing smile, Luke started the car and pulled onto Main Street. They spent the five-minute drive in silence. When he stopped in front of her house, Luke put a hand on hers.

Flinching at his touch, Hadley resisted the urge to pull her hand away. Instead, she glanced up at him.

"Sorry about the Henleys. I didn't know they'd be so rude to you, or I would never have asked you to come with me."

She shrugged. "It's okay. I'm getting used to it."

"Are you sure it wouldn't just be easier to tell them what happened?"

Hadley shook her head. Tyler was Stoneybrook's golden boy. Her ex had been their star quarterback, had taken the team to win the championship two years running. He'd bagged their groceries during his teenage years and had charmed every one of them with his handsome smile.

Part of Hadley knew there were many Stoneybrookians who wouldn't even believe Tyler had cheated on her. But even if they would believe her, Hadley didn't want to have to be the one to break it to his family. If Tyler wanted to tell them, it was up to him, but Hadley wasn't about to be the one to make them see their perfect son in anything but a glorious light.

"Ty needs to be the one to make the decision, not me," she said, hoping that would close the topic for good.

"You're a bigger person than me, then," Luke said.

"Not just more naïve?" She cocked an eyebrow at him, throwing his previous comment back at him as well.

He laughed. "I guess I deserve that. But seriously, you're a good person, Had." His blue eyes locked on to hers. "I'm sorry Tyler took advantage of that."

Speechlessness hit Hadley about as intensely as Luke's apology. It wasn't like he could've controlled Tyler's behavior as his best friend any more than she could've as Tyler's wife, but it was nice regardless. And as much as Luke liked to joke around, liked to mess with her, she could tell he meant what he said.

Which meant maybe she could read him like she used to.

"Thanks, Luke. See you around." She opened the door and slipped outside before she said anything else, because she didn't quite trust herself in that moment.

As she walked to her house, she wondered, did the fact that she could read Luke Fenton again mean he was changing, or was she?

❧ 11 ❧

Once Hadley got inside and heard Luke's truck pull away, she texted Paul and Suze and invited them over for dinner.

You had me at dinner, was Paul's reply.

Suze, slightly more discerning, asked, **Does this have anything to do with three people asking me about why you've been hanging out with Luke Fenton today? Post Office Pete seems to be under the impression you've been looking for houses together ...**

Hadley should've figured it would get around town. In fact, it was probably Deborah who'd started spreading the rumor. Texting back to let Suze know she would fill her in about all of it at dinner, Hadley started prepping for the meal.

She'd picked up some chicken from Hal's Food N Stuff the other day—scary as it sounded, the little market was locally sourced, and the meat came directly from Fenton Farms down the road—and she decided to try out a new recipe, jerk chicken kabobs. She still had a jar of her honey-sweetened peach chutney left over from last summer and wanted to use it up before making a new batch next week. Hadley also had a ton of summer squash, mushrooms, onions, and carrots from Hal's as well.

Setting to work, she stuck the wooden skewers in a water bath as she began washing and chopping up the lot, spreading the pieces on a baking sheet. Sprinkling some of the jerk spices on the veggies, she stuck them to roast low and slow in the oven while she cut up the chicken, seasoned it, and arranged it on the soaked skewers. After a quick check on the oven, she headed outside to the barbecue.

Ansel slipped out through the sliding glass door along with her, settling in a spot of evening sun bathing the nearest corner of grass while she worked. He blinked contentedly, only getting up to chase the occasional butterfly or gnat.

By the time the chicken was done—and looking decadently crispy—Hadley could smell the roasted vegetables wafting through the screen door. Upon her calling him, Ansel woke from his nap and followed her back inside. Hadley shut the back door just as she heard the front one open.

"Hello!" Suze called out as she entered the kitchen moments later. She held a bottle of wine in one hand and a pink box of what Hadley knew were Mickie's pastries in the other.

"Yum …" Hadley's eyes widened in question.

"Lavender shortbread cookies."

"I think I need to invite you over more often." Hadley laughed as she pulled on an oven mitt and proceeded to grab the pan out of the oven.

"Well, you're not getting drop nor crumb until I hear the story about how you and Luke went from despising each other to picking out houses together in the span of a few days."

Hadley sighed. "You know better than to believe everything you hear in town."

"So it's not true, then?"

"Well …" She tipped her head to one side. "We were in the same car, but viewing different houses. I think it's another one of Deborah's setup attempts."

Suze laughed. "Good ole Deborah. Remember when she tried to match me up with Mr. Moorbaker just because we both once said we enjoyed going to art museums?" Suze snatched a roasted carrot from the tray and popped it into her mouth. "Just be glad your guy wasn't two decades older than you."

Hadley smiled. "Yeah, I guess you're right."

The front door opened again and Hadley could tell it was Paul from the way his heavy boots clomped onto the wooden entryway floors as he pulled them off.

Suze looked down at her bare feet as Paul entered the kitchen. Wiggling her toes, she said, "Ugh. I can't believe you still have to wear those big boots in the summer. If I were you, I'd fight for the right to wear flip-flops."

Paul smirked. "Yeah, but flip-flops are only fun until I have to chase a perp down the street."

"Which happens *all the time* in Stoneybrook," Suze said, her tone sarcastic, yet playful.

Hadley held up a finger. "I saw him chasing Mrs. Holloway's pet pig, Porker, down Main Street last week."

The women laughed.

Crossing his arms over his chest, Paul said, "Laugh it up, but you seem to have forgotten I am investigating a serious murder. Oh, wait. I *know* you didn't forget because you two keep poking your noses into the case."

"And you're welcome for the help," Suze said, settling onto one of the barstools around Hadley's kitchen island.

Hadley began setting the table. "Seems like Sheriff M&M is actually letting you take a lead on this one."

Marc McKay—nicknamed by the locals as Sheriff M&M because of his resemblance to the hard-shell-covered chocolate candy and ironically not-so-sweet disposition—spent most of his time in Cascade Ridge, leaving Paul and Kevin in Stoneybrook to deal with most of the goings-on, only showing up quarterly or if something of note happened. When he did make an appearance, McKay treated his Stoneybrook deputies as if they were rookies, right out of the academy. The man had actually been on a mission to get rid of Paul, up until he'd been shot a few months before. Since then, it seemed like he was seeing his deputy in a different light.

"Yeah, he's doing some investigating up north, of course, but he's trusting me a lot more than he ever has." Paul nodded, and a bit of color brightened his cheeks.

"That's great." Hadley met her brother's proud gaze as she arranged the food onto serving plates. "That's way better than being able to wear sandals."

Suze stood, grabbing the wine key to open the bottle she'd brought. "Plus, who wants to be subjected to this guy's hairy Sasquatch toes anyway?" She winked at Paul before taking the open bottle over to the table.

He let out one of his deep, booming laughs and followed Suze, pulling out a chair for her and then Hadley as she brought the last plate over. For a few minutes, the three of them were consumed with dishing up, eating, and commenting on the way the spices mixed perfectly with Hadley's chutney. Once they began scooping seconds onto their plates, Paul seemed ready to turn to business.

"So what'd you find out with Luke today at the grocery store?" Paul asked, setting his napkin down.

Hadley did the same, though out of exasperation instead of intrigue. "People seriously need to get their own lives around here."

"Everyone's saying you went in, yelled at Tyler's parents, and then broke a bunch of stuff as you stormed out." Suze cocked an eyebrow, shooting Hadley an expression that said Suze knew it wasn't true, but would've been proud of her if it had been.

Spearing another roasted carrot with her fork, Hadley shook her head. "That was an accident." When Suze's jaw dropped open and Paul's eyes widened, Hadley added, "And I only knocked over a display. Nothing broke."

"I still don't get what that has to do with Charlie's death," Suze said.

So Hadley explained how they'd stumbled upon the secret pesticide garden behind the house Deborah had shown Luke, and how they'd learned Charlie had been renting it from the Henleys to earn a spot in the farmers market.

Paul's eyebrows knit together as he listened. "And you think Barry killed him to get revenge for taking out so many of his bees?"

Hadley put up both of her hands. "*I'm* not saying anything of the sort. Barry's one of my favorite people; I can't imagine him having anything to do with this." She glanced from Paul to Suze. "It was Luke. He thinks Barry should be on our suspect list … and Leo."

Raking his fingers across his almost-black beard, Paul nodded. "Well, don't worry. Both of them were already on my suspect list."

"Along with Vivian, right?" Suze asked, her tone tightening at the woman's name.

He nodded. "She lied to you, all right. Told me she knew him, but only in a professional capacity. I'm not sure what she's hiding there. Though, other than that and her presence in Stoneybrook the morning he was killed, I can't think of any motives for her to want to kill him. Both Barry and Leo had good reason to want Charlie dead, but Vivian … I don't see it."

Hadley pressed her lips together for a moment before blurting out, "I'm going to go house hunting with her, so I can do some more digging." She immediately felt better having told him. She was worried Paul would tell her not to go through with her plan, but lying to him would've been worse.

Suze watched wide-eyed as Paul's expression changed from surprise to annoyance to acceptance.

"Okay," Paul dipped his chin once.

"Did he just go through the three stages of My Sister's a Busybody that quickly?" Suze whispered in awe.

Hadley put down her fork and focused on her brother. "Seriously?"

"Seriously. You've got the perfect cover. Promise me you'll take Suze with you, though?"

The women each raised a hand and held up three fingers. "We swear," they said together, then added, "May the odds be ever in our favor."

"And the moment anything seems sketchy, you get out of there. Clear?" His voice dipped low into his *I mean it this time* range.

Keeping their hands raised, Hadley and Suze nodded. "Clear," Suze said.

"Should we look into Charlie's assistant manager

anymore while we're up there?" Hadley asked, her brother's approval of their first plan going to her head.

"Absolutely not. The sheriff or I will be questioning him further." He pointed at Hadley. "Stick to Vivian, or I'll take that away from you too."

They promised they would as Paul gathered the dirty dishes. Hadley began to pack up the leftovers, and Suze plated the dessert. Like a well-oiled, three-wheeled machine, they were each sitting down with a cookie and a refilled glass of wine within minutes.

"So … did you find any houses you liked driving around with Deborah and Luke?" Paul asked around a mouthful of cookie.

"Meh," Hadley said. "A few nice ones, but nothing with all of my look-fors."

"You'll find something, I'm sure." Suze winked at her friend.

Despite Suze's reassurance, Hadley only sighed. "I hope so. At this point, finding Charlie's killer seems like an easier task than finding me a home."

🦋 12 🦋

Vivian called the next day to set up an appointment for them to go tour a few houses Friday morning. Hadley accepted, and she and Suze set out to Cascade Ridge after grabbing their obligatory lattes.

"Hmm …" Hadley's brows knit together as she scanned through the listings Vivian had sent her on her phone.

"What?" Suze asked, glancing over, then looking back at the road as they pulled into the bustling town.

"She wasn't kidding when she said my money wouldn't go as far up here as it would down in Stoneybrook."

"They're bad?"

Hadley wrinkled her nose. "Not great." She shook her head. "What am I saying? I'm not going to buy any of these houses. What do I care if Cascade Ridge property values are ridiculously high?"

Suze chuckled as she pulled into the parking lot. "I know. I found myself getting excited this morning, thinking you might find a house today, before I remembered this is all a ruse."

With the reminder of their mission, the women walked

into the realty office. Hadley, looking forward to seeing that wonderful view out Vivian's office window, was disappointed when the woman came out with her purse and sunglasses, ready to go. She led them out to an immaculate Mercedes SUV which put Deborah's to shame.

I guess higher property values means a higher cut for her, Hadley thought, admiring the leather interior as she buckled herself into the passenger seat.

Suze slipped into the back seat while Vivian started the car, and they were off.

It was a good thing Hadley didn't want to buy a house in Cascade Ridge because if she had, she would've been sorely disappointed in what fit her budget up north. Two had garages that had been poorly converted into extra living rooms. One had a kitchen that looked like it had been created in the image of every seventies trend. And none of them had even a whisper of a view of the mountains or the valley below.

Hadley let out a long sigh as they climbed back into the SUV after the third disappointing house. Hadley shot Suze a quick glance. Now was their chance to talk with Vivian about Charlie, to try to get a little more information.

Anytime either of the Stoneybrook women had tried to bring it up earlier, Vivian had changed the topic back to either the house they were viewing or the one they were on their way to next. Having planned on bringing them to three houses today, the realtor was officially out of houses to discuss. And as Vivian started the car and headed back toward the realty office, Hadley knew she was running out of time.

"So … Vivian," Hadley said, smiling over at the woman. "Like I said, I'm selling my place down in Stoneybrook. I want it to look its best for the pictures. Any florists you might recommend to coordinate a few arrangements for me?"

Vivian answered brightly. "For sure. That's the great thing about living in a city versus a tiny township. We've got choices."

"What about Bloom?" Suze asked. "It might be nice to support the place since the owner just died. If they're staying open, that is."

At that, their driver's jaw tightened and she said, "I wouldn't patronize that establishment again if someone paid me. The owner was a con artist and I doubt anyone who worked for him is any better."

Hadley suppressed any outward sign of celebration as she took in what Vivian had just said. That sounded like motive enough for murder.

"I thought you said you didn't know the owner?" Hadley said.

Slim fingers tightening on the wheel, Vivian took a sudden right turn, taking both Hadley and Suzanne by surprise. They slid in their seats and clung to the door handles next to them.

"Sorry about that, girls. I forgot a house just lowered into your price range this morning, Hadley. I wasn't sure you would be interested, but since you didn't find anything earlier, maybe this will be helpful to look at."

Hadley was still reeling from the drastic turn. "Uh, sure."

Vivian drove down a street that had a beautiful view of both the mountains and the valley, unlike the other houses they'd seen today. Hadley blinked as the realtor pulled into the driveway of a big, beautiful craftsman home. The cedar siding was gorgeous and the white trim made everything look polished. She wasn't a professional like Vivian, but

Hadley guessed the square footage must've been in the three-thousand range. Even the yard was amazing, with pops of bright green and purples in a river-stone design.

"This is in my price range?" Hadley asked, taking it all in.

Vivian flashed her an excited smile. "At the tippy top, but it's there. Like I said, just lowered."

"How long has it been on the market?" Suze asked, a wrinkle forming in between her eyebrows.

"Only a month." Vivian's smile faltered, and she glanced down. "This time. Two years before that."

Suze pressed her lips into a thin line, eyeing Hadley in her *this is suspicious* way.

Hadley felt like rolling her eyes at her friend. Just because a house had been on the market for a while didn't mean a thing. Maybe it had been priced too high before, but Hadley doubted that after seeing the other options in her price range.

"Do you know why it's been on the market so long?" Hadley asked, humoring her best friend.

Vivian shrugged. "Honestly, it beats me. It's a little rough on the inside, but nothing someone couldn't fix with some paint and some sweat equity." Vivian opened her car door. "Shall we?"

Hadley nodded and followed her outside. Suze paused, making Hadley wonder if she was going to refuse to join them until she opened the back door and followed them up the pathway.

The views just got better the closer Hadley got to the house. She reminded herself that even if she liked this house, she was *not* moving to Cascade Ridge. *But* … her thoughts prodded as she stood on the porch and looked out over the valley to the right of the house. She could see

Stoneybrook down below, hugging the Cascade River as if it were a silvery lifeline in the green abyss.

No, Hadley scolded herself. *I'm only looking at this place to get close to Vivian. It doesn't matter that it's quite possibly my dream house.*

Suze stood next to Hadley as Vivian worked on the realtor lockbox to retrieve the key. Suze crossed her ams in front of her chest. Hadley wondered if she was sour about how nice the house was and maybe even worried Hadley might want to move in.

Vivian opened the door, and the only thing Hadley could think was Suze didn't have to worry one bit about her buying this house. While the place certainly was something that might visit a person in their sleep, it was more of a nightmare than a dream.

Immediately upon stepping foot inside, Suze wrapped her arm through Hadley's, pulling close. There was an eerie feeling hanging in the air. Hadley felt as if someone were hanging over her shoulder, breathing on her neck, and they definitely didn't have good intentions.

Inside was dark, musty, and a wreck. The people who had lived there prior—who seemed to have been long gone based on the stale, unlived-in smell—must've taken the appliances with them. The kitchen was all cabinetry bones and exposed wires.

Hadley wasn't sure if she'd ever seen carpets so dirty. She had a terrible feeling they had been a completely different color when they'd been installed. Now they seemed to resemble a puce shade, dotted with questionable stains every few feet.

"So … like I said, it needs some work inside." Vivian seemed like she was trying hard to smile, but it was coming off as more of a cringe.

"That's the understatement of the century," Suze whispered to Hadley. "I'd say it needs to be gutted, or burned."

Hadley shivered and couldn't disagree.

"The other rooms have a lot more character," Vivian said, leading them farther inside.

The women followed, if only out of a morbid sense of curiosity at that point. Unfortunately, things did not improve in the rest of the house. Vivian hadn't been wrong about the other rooms having more character, but what she'd failed to mention was how the character they had was the awful kind that made for an irredeemable villain from a horror story.

There were odd windows into other rooms, something that may have felt whimsical in a cleaner, less terrifying house, but felt like a tool murderers might use to spy on victims in this one. In each room they visited, Vivian tried to focus on the least frightening features, but Suze and Hadley looked right past them to the disturbing ones, clutching each other tighter with each new space.

And then they went into the "finished" basement.

"A finished basement is a huge plus in any listing," Vivian said, tripping on the inexplicably uneven floor.

"The only thing anyone ever *finished* in this basement is *killing people*." Suze's whispers grew frantic and high pitched. "Hadley, we need to get out of this murder house right now."

Hadley had been trying to think of ways to get Vivian talking about Charlie, but kept getting distracted by the next new and alarming room. She nodded. They needed to get out of there. The *someone's leaning over your shoulder* feeling was becoming more of a *someone's holding a knife to your throat* feeling instead. She turned to Vivian, who was still going strong with the tour even though Hadley was sure her expression looked equally as horrified as Suze's did.

"Another lovely feature is that there's access to the crawl-space underneath the house right here in the finished basement." Vivian gestured to a large, cast-iron door set into the wall.

The instinctual, animal part of Hadley's brain set alarm bells blaring the moment she locked eyes on the door. Her skin grew clammy as her inner dialogue freaked out. All she could think was, *That's no crawl space, it's where a killer stores bodies … or people who are doomed to become bodies.*

As if to prove her point, something cried out from behind the door.

Hadley's heart stopped. *Oh no. There's a ghost in here with us.*

"So, that was terrifying." Suze's voice shook as she backed up a few steps. "Just checking you two heard that as well, and whatever monster lives here isn't trying to lure me into the scary hole by myself."

Hadley swallowed, her throat suddenly dry. "No, I heard it."

Even Vivian—who seemed, up until that point, to be pretending everything inside the house was normal—gulped and nodded. "That definitely sounded like someone calling for help."

They glanced at each other as the sound happened again.

"I can't believe I'm going to do this." Hadley shook her head as she walked forward.

Her fingers shook as she reached for the heavy iron clasp that latched the scary door shut. She felt like a character in a horror film and hoped beyond hope this wasn't the moment where the whole audience screams at her to not open the door.

Just as her fingers closed on the latch, the hairs on her

arm raised as she had a terrible thought. Vivian had brought them there just after Hadley had asked the question about her knowing Charlie. What if the woman was the killer, knew they were onto her, and brought them to her murder house to trap them in the nightmare dungeon she kept in the basement?

Glancing back at the realtor, she studied the woman's face. There was a flicker of fear in the woman's face which matched Suze's—and probably Hadley's as well. She let her guard down again. The realtor was just as freaked out as they were.

Here goes nothing, Hadley thought as she wrenched open the door and held her breath.

Even though she purposely didn't breathe in, the smell of damp earth and mildew careened out at Hadley, as if it had been contained in there and was just as eager to leave. Blinking into the darkness, Hadley tried to make out shapes or anyone who might've been crying out moments before.

She jumped as something moved in the darkness.

❧ 1 3 ❧

The shape came barreling toward her in the dark. Hadley braced herself for whatever was about to happen. She wanted to slam the door closed, but was frozen on the spot as if she were a rabbit facing down a wolf.

Just when she thought she might pass out from the fear coursing through her body, Hadley focused in on the murky crawlspace, and she made out an orange creature.

"Mew." The sound was strained, like someone whose voice was failing after they've yelled too much.

The orange shape put its paws up on the edge of the doorframe, rolling wild, white-rimmed eyes at Hadley.

"Mew?" it seemed to ask this time.

"It's a kitten?" Suze asked from a safe distance behind her.

"It's a kitten." A grin pulled across Hadley's face. She felt like laughing or crying, or both, from the relief of it all. "How in the world did you get in here?" she asked the small, dirty creature as she scooped it up in her hands.

Vivian exhaled the breath she must've been holding. "I recognize you," she said, walking forward to pet the cat. "I showed this house last week, and this little one was running around outside."

"But then how'd it get in the creepy dungeon?" Suze asked.

Vivian leveled her with an exasperated look, but Suze just shrugged.

"I'm not the only one who shows this house. Maybe when someone else was touring it, the cat slipped into the crawlspace and they didn't realize it."

The kitten was purring and its eyelids fluttered as if it were already falling asleep. The poor thing must have been stressed out and scared beyond measure. Hadley held it closer. "Or someone put you in there on purpose." Her face contorted into a frown at the thought.

Neither Suze nor Vivian seemed ready to dispute that possibility, so Hadley decided something.

"I'm taking her … him?" She peered at the cat's face as if it might tell her. "This kitten is skin and bones. I don't know how it has survived up until now, but if it's been living in an abandoned house, taking it shouldn't be a problem, right?"

Vivian swiped her shoulder-length hair out of her face. "It could've belonged to the people who just vacated the house last month. They left in a hurry."

"I wonder why?" Suze asked, sarcasm dripping from her question.

Ignoring Suze, Vivian said, "We see this a lot. People aren't sure if they're going to be able to bring animals to their new residence, so they don't chance it, they leave them behind. Or they don't want to have to worry about another mouth to feed when they're on the move."

Hadley tried hard not to be judgmental of others; she knew everyone was dealing with their own problems in their own, unique circumstances. And even though she couldn't imagine ever leaving Ansel behind—even in the weeks she'd had him, he'd become an integral part of her life—she decided to assume the people who left the kitten thought it would find a better home.

Like with me, she thought to herself as she scratched its head.

"Okay, let's get out of here." Hadley turned toward Vivian. "This place gives me the creeps."

Vivian, the only one still unconvinced of the house's lack of charm—or maybe the woman was that committed to making a deal—set her jaw and led them up and out of the basement.

The kitten was asleep in Hadley's arms by the time Vivian pulled away from the house, taking them back to the realty office in awkward silence.

"I apologize that you didn't see more of what you were hoping for today," Vivian said as she parked and turned off the car.

"Oh, that's okay." Hadley smiled reassuringly. They all climbed out of the vehicle and walked into the air-conditioned foyer.

"Hadley, I'll be in touch. I'll do some more searching, and we can try again in a few days. Unless, of course, you think we could go a little higher in your budget." Vivian looked as if someone had handed her a hundred dollars and told her it was all they had to buy a house.

Consciously working to keep the smile on her face, Hadley nodded. "A few days sounds great, but let's stick with the figures I gave you."

"Will do." Vivian's tone was clipped. She turned to the receptionist. "Genevieve, will you help Miss James set up an appointment for early next week, please?" She pulled a lipstick out of her purse and popped the lid off to slick some across her lips.

Hadley didn't even hear Genevieve's reply because she was too focused on the lipstick. Vivian's was in a black, opaque plastic container with a gold, plastic strip wrapped around the middle. The tube was about as different from the pink-and-silver one Hadley found at the crime scene as a lipstick could be. Disappointed, Hadley turned her attention back to Genevieve as she clicked away at her computer, pulling up Vivian's schedule.

Vivian clicked away too, high heels ringing off the tile floor as she walked back to her office.

It was then that Genevieve noticed the kitten tucked in the crook of Hadley's arm. "Omigosh! Is that a cat?" She lifted her hands to cover her mouth.

Hadley and Suze explained how they'd come across the kitten in what Suze had dubbed The Murder House.

Eyes wide, Genevieve said, "Oh, I've heard about that place. I can't believe Vivian took you there." She lowered her voice, glancing at the hall leading to Vivian's office. "I think she sees it as a challenge."

The inkling of dissent Hadley recognized in Genevieve's statement about one of her bosses gave Hadley an idea. Who knew more about someone than their receptionist? Maybe she could get the information she couldn't get out of Vivian from Genevieve.

The woman was clicking away at her computer, remembering the job she was supposed to be doing once the story about the kitten was complete.

"Does Monday at one work for you?" she asked Hadley.

"Uh, sure." Hadley wasn't sure if she would keep the appointment, but wanted to keep her options open just in case Paul thought Vivian's motive was good enough. "Hey, maybe you can help us with something."

Genevieve glanced up from her computer screen.

"Suze here is an artist, and she's got a show coming up in about a month, but she recently had a falling out with our town's florist." Hadley leaned in close. "A messy breakup."

Suze coughed at the lie. Hadley looked over at her friend who was biting back a smile. Hadley squinted one eye, almost imperceptibly, but she knew Suze would see the *just go with it* gesture. Genevieve didn't have to know that Leo was old enough to be Suze's father.

Fully entrenched in the ruse now, Suze nodded and said, "Yeah, I was supposed to order a few arrangements for the show from him, but that *cannot* happen now. You guys must use a local company for staging, right? Is there a florist you've worked with who you'd recommend up here?"

Genevieve's face softened sympathetically. "I'm so sorry. Breakups are hard enough in general. I can't imagine having to be part of the same small town and see him all the time."

Hadley and Suze glanced at each other. Hadley knew all about the awkwardness of breaking up in a small town, even though her ex significant other had moved away, she still had to deal with his family. The kitten shifted in her arms, but sighed and settled back to sleep.

"We do have a florist we work with often, actually. Let me see …" Genevieve paged through a few files sitting in an organizer on her desktop. "Here—oh …" The young woman's face lit up out of recognition, but quickly darkened as she seemed to remember something.

She's remembering Bloom was the shop they used, but the owner just died, Hadley thought as she watched the receptionist's features change.

"Something wrong?" Suze asked.

"Um …" Genevieve pressed her lips into a tight line as her eyes refocused on the two women before her. "Sorry, it's not a big deal. I was just remembering how Vivian told me she didn't want to work with them anymore, but that was for … personal reasons. They've been great with us in the past." She passed a card across the counter toward Suze.

It was a business card for Charlie Lloyd at Bloom.

Wait, she doesn't know he's dead?

Hadley's brain had a hard time comprehending at first, but then it began to settle as she realized cities as big as Cascade Ridge operated differently than small towns. Whereas it seemed everyone in Stoneybrook knew the moment anyone did anything, someone who lived in a larger city might not know someone had died for weeks or months, if ever.

Next, Hadley's brain tackled the last part of Genevieve's statement. Vivian didn't want to use Bloom anymore for *personal* reasons. That was in complete contradiction with what Vivian had told them in the car, about how he was a crook, and she wouldn't use his business.

Suze, right there with Hadley's train of thought, leaned forward and said, "Genny. Can I call you that? Genny?" When Genevieve's cheeks turned pink and she nodded, Suze continued. "You can't just drop something like that on us and leave it. We're small-town girls. We live on gossip. What happened between Vivian and this"—she made a show of looking down at the card to read the name —"Charlie Lloyd?"

Genevieve narrowed her eyes for a moment, then shifted her gaze to the hallway once more before saying, "You *did not* hear this from me, but Vivian and the owner, Charlie, were … involved for a while. Last I heard, though, Vivian had put an end to it." Genevieve shrugged.

"What for?" Hadley asked.

Genevieve smirked in that mirthless way only employees can about their controlling bosses. "She was probably afraid her husband might find out."

Hadley felt her mouth fall open. Suze gasped next to her. "You're kidding," Suze said.

The receptionist shook her head and cocked a self-satisfied eyebrow.

"Whoa." Hadley blinked, straightening when footsteps rang out from the hallway.

A man in a well-pressed suit emerged into the foyer a few moments later, smiling brightly at Hadley and Suzanne. They thanked Genevieve for her help. It was definitely time to go.

As life-long best friends, Suze and Hadley were well versed in communicating through looks. And as they walked out the realty office doors, they turned to each other to have just such a conversation about what they'd found out. The brightness of the summer sunshine put a damper on that, and they found themselves squinting and shielding their eyes, rendering any cues moot. Even the kitten blinked awake in the blinding light.

Once they got into Suze's car and shut the doors behind them, they turned to each other, wide-eyed.

"A relationship?" Hadley moved the kitten from her arm onto her lap. "That's even better motive than a business venture gone wrong."

"It looks like trying to convince you the house was great wasn't the biggest lie Vivian told today." Suze narrowed her eyes at the building. "But did you see her lipstick? That didn't look like the one you described."

Sighing, Hadley nodded. "You're right. But who only buys one type of lipstick? I think I have three different brands in my makeup drawer at home. It doesn't *definitively* mean the one at the scene wasn't also hers."

"Yes, at home. But most women bring their favorite with them in their purse." Suze pulled her own out from her purse to prove her point.

Hadley refrained from pulling her own out from her purse. "Let's get home," she said, ignoring Suze's logic for now. "We've got a lot to share with Paul, and I need to get this little one a bath." She smiled down at the orange kitten.

❧ 14 ❧

After a trip to the vet and the groomer upon returning to Stoneybrook, Hadley, Suzanne, and the kitten headed back to Hadley's house.

The vet told Hadley the stray was a female, and she was approximately ten weeks old. He gave her the first round of kitten shots and told Hadley to return in a few weeks for the next round of shots and to get spayed. She didn't have worms—thank goodness—but did have *many* fleas. The bath she got at the groomers killed the majority of those. Hadley wasn't worried about Ansel getting fleas; she had him on year-round flea medicine since he liked to follow her outside when she gardened.

What she was mostly worried about was how Ansel was going to feel about having another cat around. Suze stayed around for the whole ordeal for emotional support. And Hadley was especially grateful for her as she set up a bed for the little orange kitten in the laundry room as Ansel sniffed and hissed on the other side of the door. Suze was chatting with him, trying to calm him down.

Both the vet and the groomer had recommended a slow

introduction, putting the new cat in a room for a day or two so Ansel could get used to her smell before they met in the fur.

So far, it didn't seem to be working. Hadley frowned, but then let it pull back into a smile as the kitten curled up in the soft bed she'd made out of a towel. She would go get the kitten her own bed tomorrow, but they'd been out too long as it was, and she could see the poor little thing just needed to sleep. After being poked, and prodded, and pampered, she looked exhausted.

Once she made sure there was plenty of food and water available, Hadley slipped out of the laundry room. The kitten's eyes fluttered closed as she watched her go. Ansel glared up at her as if she'd betrayed him.

"Oh, don't look at her like that." Suze tapped her foot on the kitchen floor, snapping his attention back to her. "She's just taking in another poor soul like she did when she got you."

Smiling, Hadley knelt to let Ansel smell the kitten on her hands. He didn't hiss, but he backed away a few steps.

"I'm sorry, buddy. She needed a home. I don't want you to be stressed, though. If you're still unhappy with her tomorrow, I'll try to find another home for the little gal, okay?"

Ansel ruffled his sleek, black fur and sniffed. He sauntered away to lie in a beam of sunshine next to a tower of boxes Hadley had only half packed.

She let out an exasperated breath and looked at Suzanne.

"He'll get over himself. You'll see." She waved a hand toward the cat, dismissing his attitude.

"I hope so. The two of us have gotten along so well so far. I would hate to throw a wrench in it."

"Well, like you said, if he doesn't change his mind, you can always find someone else to take her. The most important thing was getting her out of there."

"Right," Hadley said and let that settle her worries for now.

Before they could change the subject, the sound of the front door opening alerted them to Paul's presence.

"Talk around town is you're becoming a true cat lady, Had." Paul began talking before he even entered the kitchen. When he did, he scanned the room, presumably looking for the second cat.

"Watch it, bro." Hadley pointed at him in warning. "If Ansel doesn't warm up to her, you're going to be my first choice for alternate placement. But wait … maybe she's not allowed to stay with you either."

Hadley felt like slapping her hand over her mouth. She hadn't meant to say so much, but she was tired and a little cranky. Cascade Ridge had a way of doing that to her.

Paul scoffed. "I never said you couldn't—"

"You didn't have to." She shook her head.

"Had, I'm sure he didn't—" Suze started.

"It's not just him either," Hadley said, interrupting her. "You've been odd too."

Suze looked down at her feet and Paul focused on a nonexistent spot on the kitchen counter.

Hadley watched them closely, sure she would be able to get to the bottom of whatever was going on with them. *With them.* Her mind latched on to those two words. Could it be possible that something was finally going on between them romantically? She stifled the flare of happiness that came at the thought. *No, I would be the first one they'd tell if that ever happened*, she realized, thinking about how much she'd always wanted her two best friends to be a couple. There would be no reason for them to hide it from their biggest cheerleader.

It had to be something else.

They each began spouting their own excuses. Paul was stressed, Suze tired. It was nothing. Really. Hadley's stomach dropped as she took in their expressions, their stories. Sure, she could tell something was up, but she still didn't have a clue what it was or why they would need to keep it from her.

Great. She could read Luke Fenton now, but not her brother and her best friend?

"Just forget it, both of you. I'm sorry I brought it up," Hadley said, frustrated. "Plus, we've got some information you're going to want about the case," she said to Paul, walking over to the couch and plopping herself into it.

Suze was already standing near the armchair, so she sat in that while Paul came around and settled on the opposite end of the couch from Hadley.

"I'm listening," he said.

They spilled all they'd learned about Vivian and her rumored affair with Charlie.

"Love and lust are good motives for murder, for sure." Paul rubbed the back of his neck as he seemed to be thinking through the implications of what they'd told him. "Okay, I think that's enough to get McKay involved. I'll ask him if we can go in and question her."

"Any movement with the other suspects?" Suze asked.

"Leo doesn't have an alibi other than he was setting up for the market. He was back and forth, though, and everyone is always so focused on their own booths it would've been easy for him to slip away and go over to Charlie's van."

"And Barry?" Suze asked.

Paul sighed. "Pretty much the same story as with Leo.

Barry was at the market setting up, so he had just as much opportunity as Leo."

"The difference between Leo and Barry, though, is Barry has access to the murder weapon." Hadley cringed at the unavoidable truth.

"Yeah, I'd say both of them have an equal reason to want Charlie dead, but Barry has bees at his disposal." Suze's face wrinkled into a frown.

"I just can't …" Paul paused. "Barry seems like the last person who would use bees as weapons. He keeps honey-bees, which means they die when they sting. I can't see that man sacrificing more of his bees just to teach someone a lesson, whether he meant to kill him or not."

"Can you send the bees found in the van to a lab some-where to figure out if they're the same kind Barry keeps?" Hadley leaned forward. When Paul agreed and wrote it on his list, she added, "That brings up something else that doesn't make sense to me. How would Barry know Charlie was deathly allergic to bees in the first place? He barely knew the guy."

"Leo would've been much more likely to know, given their history together," Suze said.

"Or, the person who makes even more sense is someone who was romantically involved with him." Hadley tipped her head to one side. "Vivian makes the most sense to me."

Suze snapped her fingers. "If he was having an affair, maybe his wife or Vivian's husband found out! We need to put them on the suspect list as well."

Taking it all in, Paul nodded. "I'll let the sheriff know to question Vivian's husband about his whereabouts, but I know he already cleared Charlie's ex-wife. She was out to brunch with friends and the restaurant staff. If she's his ex-wife, and has been for some time, it takes away most of her motive. I'll dig deeper into Vivian's relationship with Charlie and see if we can analyze the bees. I think there's an entomology department at Northern Washington University we might be able to send them to," he said, naming the university just over the mountains in Pine Crest.

"Speaking of M&M," Suze said, "who does he think the killer is?"

Paul's face tightened. "He's convinced it's Barry. He won't say it outright until he has definitive proof, but I can tell that's what he's betting on."

"Did you tell him what you said to us about Barry hurting bees?" Hadley's voice cracked around the question, scared for her favorite beekeeper.

Her brother nodded. "I did, but I didn't push him. He's letting me take more of a lead on this case, something he's never let me do before, and I don't want to ruin it. Plus, I think I can do more to help Barry and Leo by finding who actually did it rather than arguing with McKay."

Hadley chewed on her lip, but conceded he was right.

"I think you're right." Suze smiled at Paul. "The best thing we can do is to focus on finding the real killer."

"You've got a long list of stuff there." Hadley pointed to the pad sitting next to her brother. "What can we do to help?"

Paul scratched his forehead, his signature stalling-for-time move. Though he let the two civilians help out, he was careful about what he let them do.

"If you two could figure out what kind of bees Barry keeps, it would be helpful to know for when we get information back about the ones that killed Charlie," he said finally.

The women agreed, and Hadley held back her excitement at having a job to do, knowing it was nice of Paul to let them be involved at all.

"Okay." Paul stood, tucking the pad of paper into his back pocket. "I'd better get going."

"Me too," Suze said, following suit. "I've got some work to catch up with after all our sleuthing." She shot a smirk in Hadley's direction.

Hadley only groaned. "I've got packing to do. So much packing."

"You'll find a house. Don't worry," Paul said with a reassuring pat on her shoulder.

"Thanks," she said, waving goodbye as they left.

When she turned around, Ansel was back at the laundry room door, hissing and pacing. Sighing, she went over to try to calm him down. She sank to the kitchen floor, petting him as he climbed into her lap.

"Maybe bringing the kitten home was just another in a series of terrible ideas I've had lately, huh buddy?"

Even though he purred, the cat glared as he blinked up at her with his amber eyes.

❧ 15 ❧

The next day was cloudy and muggy. Suze and Hadley weren't the only slow-to-move vendors that morning as they set up for the Saturday market. By the time she sat down in the chair behind her jam table, Hadley's T-shirt clung to her uncomfortably. She couldn't tell whether or not to wear her sunglasses to block out the white glare the clouds created.

It was a good thing they still had a few minutes before the market opened. Hadley needed to cool down a little before she was expected to talk to customers.

"Any changes with the felines?" Suze asked, swiping sweat off her forehead.

Hadley shook her head. "Nope. If anything, it's worse. Ansel hissed at me this morning when I tried to move him away from the laundry room door."

"And Miss Kitten?"

"She's gotten over being tired and has now become playful. She seems upset being cooped up in that tiny laundry room."

Hadley couldn't believe the amount of stress she'd

created for herself by bringing the kitten home. She'd thought she was doing the right thing, and it had backfired completely.

"You know, Paul's not your only option if you don't want to keep her." Suze arched an eyebrow.

"You want a cat?" Hadley asked. "I thought you were a dog person?"

Suze had said as much on many occasions, which was why Hadley hadn't even thought of her when they'd found the kitten yesterday.

"I am a dog person." Suze fanned her face with one of the signs for her table. "I didn't mean me. There are tons of cat lovers in Stoneybrook. And people love kittens." She shrugged.

Hadley pressed her lips together. "Oh. Right. Yeah." She bobbed her head in agreement, but deep down knew she didn't want to give the kitten away. Last night, she'd gone into the laundry room to sit with her for a little while so she wouldn't get lonely. She was not only cute as pie, but super sweet to boot. She'd given Hadley about a million head boops, all while purring up a storm.

"But ...?" Suze smirked.

"I like her. A lot."

"So give it time."

Hadley agreed as customers began walking through the market.

They were quite busy for the first hour—Hadley barely had a chance to catch her breath in between customers. But she managed to sell out of all of her stock in that hour. The peach lavender jam she'd made on a whim had been a big hit. She put up her "Sorry, sold out!" sign, glad she'd made it for the few times a year such an event took place.

"Hey, I'm gonna go shop around," she told Suze as she

headed toward the beginning of the market. Suze waved as she rang up a customer buying a dozen of her printed cards.

It was funny that such a cloudy day would bring out so many shoppers. When she'd first started selling at the market, Hadley expected the sunniest days to be the busiest. But it was often the opposite. Pure, sunny days in the valley often stole customers off on hikes, bike or horseback rides, or river rafting. Rainy days weren't great for crowds either, but it was those overcast days which tended to be the biggest moneymakers.

Toward the market entrance, Hadley spotted Barry's honey stand and noticed he was without customers at the moment. She remembered, all too late, that she was supposed to come up with a way to inconspicuously figure out what kind of bees Barry kept. Instead, she'd been too focused on the kitten and packing. Wracking her brain as she walked forward, she tried to make it up on the spot.

I could tell him I'm doing research for … No. Maybe if I tell him I want to keep my own bees? Or would he just see me as competition? Her thoughts raced for a solution as she closed in on his booth.

Then she overheard a customer standing in front of Wendy's coffee cart tell her husband, "Honey, doppio is just a fancy way of saying decaf."

Wendy said, "Actually, doppio is a double shot of espresso." She winked at Hadley as she noticed her passing by.

The woman's gentle correction caused a light bulb to go off in Hadley's brain. That was it! She loved talking to customers about the difference between jams, jellies, and preserves whenever they asked her, or—on certain occasions —when they called her jams preserves. The corrections were never borne from a frustration with the customer, but rather an excitement about her craft.

An excitement she knew her fellow vendors shared for their creations.

Barry smiled up at her as she stepped up to his booth. His wild, white hair framed his wrinkled face. "Morning, darling." Lovely crow's-feet appeared next to his brown eyes as he greeted her.

Hadley's heart stepped in the way, almost blocking her from her mission from Paul. The man was the sweetest and had never been anything but supportive and lovely to her.

Finding out the truth is helping him, she reminded herself with a steadying breath.

"Hi, Barry." Hadley picked up her favorite blend of his honey, knowing she'd need more to make another batch of the honey chutney, and handed him cash for her purchase.

Thinking one more moment about her plan, she decided on the untruth she would use to bait the man into a conversation.

"I have to tell you, I learned the coolest thing the other day, Barry."

He leaned forward in anticipation. "You don't say."

She nodded. "I learned there's a certain type of honeybee that dances." A smile overcame her features as she remembered the first time she'd seen a video of the waggle dance which bees used to communicate the location of flowers to their hive.

Hadley's grin was mirrored on Barry's face. "Actually," he said, "most types of honeybees have their own dialect of a dance-like form of communication."

She chewed the inside of her cheek to hold her smile from getting any bigger as he took the bait. "Interesting. I saw a video of it. They were so cute, wiggling around. The bees in the video were a lot darker than the average honeybee, though. I just figured it was specific to that kind."

Barry ran a hand through his white beard. "A darker bee might be Russian. I'd have to see it to tell for sure."

"Are those the kind of bees you keep?"

"Oh, I've always kept Italian honeybees. They're what my father kept, and we tend to stick with what we know, right?"

Hadley agreed. "Well, now I learned a second thing. Russian, Italian. I didn't know bees came from so many different places."

"There are also Carniolan, Buckfast, Caucasian, and German." He beamed, obviously loving a chance to share his knowledge with a willing listener.

"Well, thank you. For the honey and the information." She held up the jar and waved as she left him.

Dropping the jar off at her own table, Hadley checked in with Suzanne now that she was done helping her customer.

"Italian bees," she told her after she explained how she'd gotten Barry to talk.

Suze frowned. "Aww. I can't believe you went sleuthing without me."

"Sorry." Hadley wrinkled her nose. "I just got excited. But you can help me with the next part."

"Next part?" Suze narrowed her eyes. "Paul just said to find out about the bees."

Hadley put a hand on her hip. "Since when do we do everything Paul says?"

Suze swallowed, but then grinned. "Right. What's the plan?"

Hadley eyed the Valley Wildflowers booth down by the Fenton Farms stand. Jessie stood behind the table instead of Leo. It wasn't unusual for Jessie to help out in her dad's shop or in his place at the market, but this time felt different.

Between his absence in the shop on Monday and a lone Jessie today, it felt to Hadley as if he were hiding.

"We're going to question Jessie and see if we can't get her to tell us the real reason her dad hasn't been around since Charlie was killed."

"Both of us at once? But who will watch our stands?" Suze asked.

Hadley's scheming smirk fell flat. While she had sold out of her jams, Suze still had prints and a few originals left. She didn't want her friend to miss out on any sales. Because she was a good friend, Hadley said, "I got to talk to Barry, you take Jessie. I'll stay here."

Suze smiled a thank you and was about to head that way when Potholder Penny walked over from the next booth.

"You two looking for Leo, I hear." The middle-aged woman snapped gum as if she were a teenager at the mall.

Hadley crossed her arms in front of her. "You eaves-dropping again, Penny?"

Penny put up her hands as she said, "I can't help it if you're talking super loud." The problem with the gesture was that she was still wearing a potholder on each of her hands as she often did to model their design.

The sight of her standing there, potholder-covered hands raised, made Hadley and Suze sputter with barely contained laughter. Penny didn't seem to find it as funny as they did, so they composed themselves as well as humanly possible and concentrated on her first statement.

"Do you know where Leo is?" Hadley asked, wiping happy tears from her eyes.

Lowering her mitts, Penny folded them in front of her. "I heard he skipped town because he's the one who put those bees into Charlie's van."

Luckily, Hadley and Suze had Paul, so they knew better

than to believe obvious untruths such as that statement. Paul had been in to question Leo himself. The man hadn't run away. But he was hiding something.

"You really think he did it?" Suze asked, leveling her most dubious gaze on Penny.

Penny slapped a mitted hand over her heart. "Me? I don't think he did. I'm just hearing a lot of talk and there are people out there who think he did."

"Okay, so these people—who are definitely not you—" Hadley said, "what are they saying is the reason behind why Leo killed Charlie?"

"Wedding Gate, of course." Penny leaned forward as she whispered, her eyes widening.

What Penny was referring to was, of course, the scandal that had taken place around Christmas last year when Leo had landed a high-end client from Seattle through a wedding expo. The young woman had been from an affluent family, deeply entrenched in the coffee capitol's social scene. Her wedding was to be featured in all of the popular Northwest bridal magazines and would've been amazing for publicity.

Charlie, who'd been at the same expo, had tracked her down once she'd left the Valley Wildflowers table. He'd convinced her there was a new strain of beetle which was ravaging the Cascade Valley and even he wouldn't have taken her on as a client because the beetles were ruining the flowers. He implied that Leo might very well destroy her wedding day with these hole-filled, infested flowers. The girl was as gullible as she was rich, it turned out, and she went straight back to Leo and canceled her appointment. Charlie hadn't stopped there, doing the same thing to the next two clients, all three of them canceling even after Leo assured them it was a lie.

Leo had been crushed, but even more than that, he had been furious.

"But Wedding Gate was six months ago. Why would Leo wait until now to get his revenge?" Suze asked.

Penny waggled her eyebrows as if she were a Marx brother who'd just spotted a pretty girl. "That's the interesting thing. Thea Clark just told me she saw Leo's flower shop listed on a realty site. Then, after Charlie showed up dead, the listing disappeared."

Hadley and Suze glanced at each other. They'd known about the shop being up for sale, but Hadley hadn't gone back to see whether or not it still was. It was entirely plausible that Leo had gotten to the point where he had to put his business up for sale, had blamed it on Charlie, and killed him to get revenge. Or maybe Leo thought he would have to sell the place if Charlie was going to compete with him, but with the other flower seller out of the picture, he would get to stay open.

"That does kinda change things," Hadley admitted.

Suze nodded. "Which makes it extra important that I go talk with Jessie and ask her if she knows why her dad has been keeping a low profile."

Hadley agreed, but just as Suze started to leave for the florist's booth, Hadley saw something that made her simultaneously freeze and grow uncomfortably warm. She reached out and gripped Suze's arm, stopping her just before she could step away.

"Suze, I'm sorry, but you're not going anywhere."

Suze followed Hadley's intense gaze to the Fenton Farms stand.

"Oh boy. This is not good."

Hadley shook her head as she stared at her ex-husband.

H adley blinked, just to make sure she was seeing things clearly.

Tyler. Back in Stoneybrook. Why?

As if reading her mind, Suze whispered, "Why is Tyler here?" Being that her question was backed by surprise and anger, it came out louder than she probably meant it to.

Hadley's chest ached. She shook her head, not knowing the answer to Suze's question. Penny, having spotted Tyler, backed away to the safety of her potholders.

Tyler's dark hair had grown out since Hadley last saw him, close to five months ago. He was letting it grow out, like he used to when they were in high school. His tall, lean frame looked even more so in the dark jeans and black T-shirt he wore. It seemed as though Seattle had worn off on him in a few months, in a way it hadn't on Luke in a decade.

Speaking of Luke, he glanced over at Hadley, worry written as clear as a summer's day in his blue eyes. He pushed back his shoulders, like he always did when he was uncomfortable, then focused on Tyler again. It took a moment for Hadley to recognize Luke's anxious tell because the man was always so laid back—maddeningly so, in fact—rarely showing anything other than confidence.

Threading her arm through Hadley's, Suze pulled close. "What do you want to do? Run? Stand up to him? Stand long enough to kick him and then run? Just let me know, and I'm there with you."

Hadley smiled. Suze's undying support lightened the anvil-like weight sitting on her chest. She wished her brother could be here with her too. Then she would have her full support team surrounding her. But she'd known this moment would come. Even though Tyler had moved away, his entire family still lived here. She knew he would visit; it just felt like that time had come much sooner than she had anticipated.

"I can do this," she said, more for herself than Suze. "It's just Tyler."

"Yeah, just the man you were with for over a decade, who betrayed your trust by sleeping with someone else, and spending most of your money on her," Suze said as she stared at Tyler.

Hadley threw a sidelong glance at her friend.

"Uh, sorry. Not helpful. Got it." She nodded, then tightened the link between them as she watched Tyler turn and look in their direction.

The two women pulled in synchronized breaths, but Hadley was sure Suze's heart didn't ache as much as hers did when Tyler's dark eyes met hers.

There was a good reason he was Stoneybrook's golden boy. He'd been the high school's best quarterback in two decades—matched with Luke as his wide receiver, they'd been an unstoppable force for those few years. But it had been more than that. Tyler's good nature, devastating grin, and ability to smooth talk the wrinkles out of a rhino made it almost impossible not to like him.

Almost.

Hadley had found plenty of reasons over the past year. Which was why she kept her face passive as he hit her with that famous smile and headed over. Glancing behind him at Luke, Hadley noticed his friend adjust his shoulders again as he feigned interest in a row of corn on the cob.

Tyler held out his arms as he approached. "Had, how ya been?" He moved to pull her into a hug as if nothing was wrong between them, as if they were the best of friends.

Luckily, Hadley's actual best friend had her back—or, her front, actually—and Suze swiveled in between the two of them, creating an awkward, three-person hug sandwich.

Tyler laughed and pulled away. He'd grown the beginnings of a beard too, Hadley noticed. He'd always stayed clean-shaven. She liked the five-o'clock shadow look on him.

"Hey, Ty. What are you doing in town?" Hadley asked, deliberately pressing her lips together so her mouth wouldn't hang open in her surprise.

"Accounting business. I still have clients in town, you know."

"You couldn't do that from Seattle?" Suze asked, crossing her arms.

"And miss seeing my favorite Stoneybrook girl?" He grinned, but the smile faded as he glanced behind Hadley.

"Favorite? Tyler, you and I have very different ways of showing favoritism." Paul's voice was low and menacing as he stepped up next to Hadley.

She felt like crying with relief. He had heard her twin-connection plea for help. Or it was possible he'd just stopped by the market like he often did, but Hadley liked to believe he'd sensed she needed him.

Tyler straightened his shoulders and cleared his throat. "Hey, Paul. How's it going?"

Paul cocked an eyebrow. "Oh, you know. Trying to solve a murder while supporting Hadley as she packs up the house you two used to share. What about you?"

Wrinkling his forehead, Tyler attempted to stare down the larger, hairier James twin.

"I'm … uh—" Tyler attempted, then shifted one expensively booted foot. "My mom called and … I wanted to come to town to see everyone."

Paul glared at his ex-brother-in-law.

"And Leo asked me to come talk with him about his financial options."

"Options?" Hadley asked.

Tyler's face belied his surprise. "Yeah," he said. "I mean, the man's business is …" Tyler shrugged. "Let's just say he needed a little help."

Hadley, Paul, and Suze glanced at each other.

Tyler had been in the big city for too many months it seemed. He'd forgotten the cardinal Stoneybrook rule: Always pretend you don't know what you know until the person you're talking to confirms they already know what you know, and then you can chat about it to your heart's content knowing neither of you is technically spreading gossip since you both heard it elsewhere before.

His face turned red as he realized his mistake. Hadley had learned that even in the smallest towns, secrets would always still lurk, and it wasn't smart to assume anyone knew everything. Tyler had obviously not learned the same lesson. And he'd just spilled something big.

"Is that why you're visiting?" Paul asked. "You're helping Leo with his finances?"

Tyler hadn't followed his parents into the grocery business, something that had been a real fight at the time, but most of his family had put it behind them at that point. Being an accountant, however, seemed much more lucrative in a big city rather than a small town. He was still willing to come home to bail out an old friend, it appeared.

"I didn't—I can't—" Tyler stammered, backing up a few steps as he tried to dig himself out of the mess he'd piled on.

Hadley knew it probably made her a bad person, but she got some pleasure out of watching the man squirm. He'd always been so cool, so together; even in the midst of their divorce he'd maintained the same air about him. It was nice to see he wasn't always as put together as he seemed.

But as soon as it came, the cruel thought left Hadley. Tyler may have treated her poorly, and he may have lost her trust, but he also didn't deserve to get the fifth degree his first day back in town.

"Plus," Tyler added. "I thought I could help with getting the house ready. You've got a lot going on with your business, Had."

Blinking back her surprise, Hadley was momentarily speechless. Tyler wanted to help? Also, he'd never referred to jam-making as her business. He'd always brushed it off and talked about it like it was some sticky hobby of hers.

Who was this person standing in front of her?

"Well, thanks. That would be great, actually." She found her voice.

While Tyler had already taken small things like his clothes and daily items with him when the divorce had finalized, there were still large pieces of furniture from his family and photo albums they needed to decide how to split up. Hadley had to admit having Tyler's help felt like it took a big weight off her shoulders.

Tyler's smooth facade returned and he winked at Hadley. "Anything for you, Had."

Anything except fidelity and fiscal responsibility, Hadley thought. She felt Paul shift next to her. Suze cleared her throat.

"Oh, hey. There's Jeff," Tyler said as he spotted his cousin. "I'm going to go catch up. I'll be in touch, Had." He waved as he left.

Once Tyler was gone, Hadley's tunnel vision widened, and she began to notice the rest of the market again. And while the shoppers kept going about their business as usual, all of the locals were staring in her direction. About half of the gazes were sympathetic, paired with a head tip to the side, and the other half were glares.

The sting of their split had faded in her memory and throughout the town, and Hadley had almost forgotten how it had been when she and Tyler had first told his family, and consequently the town, about their plans to divorce. But she was reminded all too clearly of how half the town wouldn't speak to her for months after and blamed her for *forcing Tyler to leave*, as went the story they'd told themselves.

Her ex-husband's return to town had seemed to rekindle the hatred and pity some of her neighbors and fellow business owners felt toward her.

Hadley glanced over at the Fenton Farms booth and noticed Luke had been watching her too. He quickly pretended to be ringing up a customer, but she saw through the act.

What does Luke think about Tyler coming home?

He had told her that he'd been upset with Tyler for cheating on her, had even told him to stop. But Luke and Tyler had been friends since forever. Of course Luke's loyalty would lie with Tyler over Hadley. She was fooling herself to think them getting along better lately might mean anything different.

She turned to face Paul and Suze. "Thanks, you two. I don't know how I would've gotten through that without you."

Suze reached forward to grab Hadley's hand, squeezing it tight in hers.

"Anytime I can take that jerk down a peg, I'm happy." Paul stepped closer, wrapping an arm around Hadley's shoulders and pulling her into a hug. "You're a way nicer person than I am."

"I say that about her all the time." Suze chuckled, but then pointed at them. "I think Had may be too nice for her own good, though."

Hadley felt her cheeks heat up as Paul stepped back, releasing her from the hug. She looked down at her hands, noticing with a groan that she shouldn't have bothered applying new nail polish last night as most of it was now chipped off.

Around them, the market was beginning to wind down, though there was still a good two hours left. Hadley swiped a hand over her face, trying to reset it from the confused frown she felt like it had frozen in.

"I think I might pack up early and head home, if that's okay with you, Suze." Hadley met her friend's gaze.

Suze's face softened. "Of course. You go. I can find my own way back. Penny can give me a ride since she owes me a favor after I showed her how to create that blog she's been wanting to start forever," Suze said, raising her voice on the last part and leaning forward so Penny could hear her.

Their neighbor rolled her eyes, but nodded reluctantly.

"Or I can stay and help," Paul said. When both Hadley and Suze looked at him in surprise, he added, "I could use a little time around the locals to do some questioning for this case. I can take Suze back in my truck."

"That would be great." Hadley smiled and began packing up. "Oh, by the way," she said, turning to Paul. "Barry keeps Italian bees."

He thanked her and said he would let the sheriff know.

Once Hadley dropped off her supplies at the jam kitchen, she hopped on her bike to head back home. The ride through the cool breeze and sunshine served to calm her worries and lighten her spirit, so by the time she reached her house, she was feeling like she was finally letting go of Tyler's sudden reappearance.

All sense of calm left her as she walked into the kitchen. Ansel was perched like an angry gargoyle outside of the laundry room, glaring as if he had killer eye-lasers that might penetrate the door and destroy the kitten for good.

Hadley felt like crying. "Ansel, can't you just get along with her? This is the last thing I need today."

The black-and-white cat growled at the door in response.

"Maybe if you could just see her," Hadley said. "Would that make it better?"

He licked his paw.

"Well, it's worth a try."

At the end of her rope, Hadley carefully opened the laundry room door and picked up the orange kitten. She was waiting just on the other side and mewed when she saw Hadley's face.

Then, sitting on the kitchen floor, Hadley set the kitten in her lap as she crossed her legs under her. Ansel growled louder.

"Or this will make it worse," Hadley whispered to

herself and rubbed her thumbs into her temples, feeling a headache coming on from all of the stress.

While Hadley's hands were busy kneading her temples, the kitten jumped free of her lap and scrambled over to where Ansel crouched. His growls deepened and grew louder the closer the kitten came.

Hadley's breath caught in her throat. The kitten was fast. She was already standing in front of Ansel by the time Hadley could react and shoot forward to grab her.

But before Hadley could get to the kitten, Ansel's growls broke into a full hiss. The kitten, seemingly undeterred, took another step closer so she was right in front of the angry cat. Then, without warning, her small paw whipped forward, smacking Ansel right in the face.

The growling and hissing came to a sudden halt. Ansel blinked in surprise.

Hadley stood there, poised to grab him if he decided to retaliate, but she found she didn't need to worry. The look of surprise on Ansel's face was quickly replaced with interest. He leaned forward and smelled the kitten, who was still standing her ground. Then he licked her face.

The kitten walked forward and head-butted the older cat, rubbing her body against his. Hadley relaxed. She couldn't help but grin as the sound of purring met her ears. Ansel began following the kitten around as she explored the rest of the kitchen.

Sighing, Hadley enjoyed having at least one of the problems in her life resolved.

❧ 17 ❧

The next day, Hadley called up Vivian's receptionist and canceled her Monday appointment with the woman, stating she would call and set up another time when she could. With Tyler in town, Hadley just couldn't fathom adding anything more to her plate. It seemed as if she'd learned as much as she could from Vivian, anyway.

Minutes after she hung up with one realty office, her other realtor called. Deborah had found a house she thought was The One for Hadley. Seeing as how Deborah had said that a few times already, Hadley didn't get too excited, but she did agree to be ready in half an hour to go look at it.

She didn't even feel guilty about leaving for however long it took to go see the house. Between last night and that morning, Hadley had managed to pack up all of the nonessentials in her bedroom and create a pile of things she needed to go through with Tyler. It had been her most productive packing day yet. Knowing Tyler would be there to help had made a world of difference, and having the cats get along like long-lost siblings didn't hurt.

It was a particularly hot day, with temperatures creeping into the nineties as noon approached, and not a cloud in the vast blue sky. Hadley changed out of her dusty packing clothes and slipped into her favorite floral cotton dress. She plaited her long, dark hair into a side braid, which fell over her left shoulder.

Half an hour later, she was soaking up the midday sun as she stood in front of her house, waiting for Deborah. She lifted her face to the warmth, smiling and leaning back against her fence for support. Hadley was just contemplating whether or not she should pop back inside to put on another layer of sunscreen when Deborah pulled up.

Hadley jumped a little in surprise as she noticed Luke sitting in the back seat when she climbed inside. His lips quirked into a half smile and he waved.

Noticing Hadley's surprise, Deborah said, "Oh, I'm sorry I didn't mention it on the phone, but Luke called this morning and had a property he wanted to see right around the same area I'm taking you. I didn't ask since you two seemed to be getting along so well last time. I figured it would be okay."

The setup attempt was back on, it appeared. Hadley feigned a smile. *Yeah, but last time was before his best friend came back into town and reminded me of why we don't get along*, she thought to herself. Aloud, she said, "Oh, sure. That's fine. Hey, Luke." Hadley didn't look back at him. She buckled in, focusing forward.

Deborah looked a little disappointed at the lackluster greeting, but started driving anyway.

The awkward air between Hadley and Luke felt almost palpable, and maybe it was, because after the first five minutes, Deborah said, "I saw Tyler's back in town, Hadley. How are you feeling about that?"

Was Deborah onto a new setup, or was she thinking it might make Luke jealous?

Shrugging, Hadley said, "He's just visiting, but I'm fine. He's going to help me get the house ready, which I appreciate."

Deborah waggled an eyebrow in Hadley's direction. "Oh, I see. Having a big, strong man around to help with the heavy lifting can't hurt."

Unsure whether she wanted to burst out laughing or hide her face in embarrassment, Hadley squeaked out a, "Deborah!"

The woman grinned conspiratorially. "What? It can't. Plus, with a history like the two of you have, you never know what could happen when you two get all sweaty moving boxes."

Yep. New setup, for sure.

This time Hadley did laugh. "Hold your horses, woman. Nothing's going to happen. We're 100 percent divorced." She shot a *can you believe this woman?* look back at Luke, but he was staring out the window.

Deborah patted Hadley's hand. "You keep telling your-self that, dear. As someone who's been divorced before, I can tell you the spark never dies out. It's always burning somewhere, however small. Like a pilot light, if you will." She pulled into a vacant lot. "And here we are, Luke."

Luke was out the door before Deborah even turned off the car. He strode around the property for a few minutes while Deborah jogged behind him, reading him stats off the listing. Hadley stayed in her seat, but rolled down her window after the air inside became stifling after a few minutes.

"You could build in a variety of spots on this property, but I think this over here would be the best spot since you get a great view of the mountains, especially if you build something that's a few stories tall." Deborah squinted in the sunlight and pointed to a flat part of the clearing to their right.

Nodding, Luke appeared to relax out of the uptight mood he'd seemed to be in when they'd first arrived. "It's a good option. I've been thinking more about building."

They chatted about his options for a few more minutes and then returned to the vehicle.

"It's nice out here, Luke," Hadley said once the others were back inside the car with her.

He didn't even meet her gaze as he buckled in and grunted out a response.

Surprised, Hadley focused on rolling up her window as Deborah started the car and the AC turned on again. Then she spent the five-minute drive to the next property completely chipping the nail polish off her left pointer finger.

What was Luke's problem?

She didn't have a chance to dwell on the question, because they arrived at the house Deborah had brought her to see.

"Wait, this is Leo's rental." Hadley blinked as they drove down the oak-lined driveway and stopped in front of the beautiful, cedar-shake house. She looked over at Deborah. "I didn't know he was selling."

Deborah's bright red lips curled into a smirk. "It's not even on the market yet. He owes me a favor, so he told me about it first."

Hadley couldn't help but return Deborah's smile. After downsizing to a smaller house once his daughter went off to college last year, the whole town had been watching what Leo would do with his house. Still unsure what his future held, he'd decided to rent it out, much to the disappointment of the dozen or more townspeople who'd had their eye on the place for the past decade.

No one thought he would ever part with the place. He had called it his refuge, the house he'd purchased after he and his wife had divorced when Jessie was a child.

A single dark cloud darkened Hadley's excited thoughts as she looked out at her dream house. She couldn't help but recall how Tyler had let slip the fact Leo's business was in trouble. Was that part of the reason he'd decided to sell his other house? Was he selling this place instead of the store? She remembered Penny mentioning the store was no longer for sale. The thought sat in her gut like a pill taken on an empty stomach.

Hadley chanced a glance back at Luke. "Can you believe this?" she asked.

He shook his head, surprise lifting whatever odd mood he'd gotten himself into earlier.

"Let's go look!" Deborah clapped her hands excitedly.

The three of them exited the car. Hadley sighed as the sound of the river enveloped them from where it rushed by at the bottom of a ravine to her right. It was the perfect location: a short walk downhill to the banks, but without having to worry when the river occasionally flooded during the rainy months in the spring and fall.

The property was dotted with old-growth pine trees, enough to throw patches of shade on the house and yard, but not enough to block a good splashing of sunlight.

"As you probably know, the house is just under twenty-four hundred square feet. The deck adds another seven hundred to that, if you consider it an extension of the living space, which I do."

Deborah led them inside.

The whole house smelled like laundry dried in the summer breeze. Whitewashed walls accentuated the dark wood moldings and accent beams. Sunlight streamed into the kitchen through multiple skylights in the celling, bathing the painted concrete countertops in warmth.

"Is there still a tenant here?" Hadley asked, pointing to a bag visible in the open bedroom and a makeup bag sitting on the counter of the guest bathroom.

Deborah waved a hand. "Jessie's just staying here for now. Probably wanted her own space since she's so used to living away from her dad now." The woman rolled her eyes, letting them know exactly what she thought of that.

She bustled them down the hall and into the great room.

"There are three bedrooms, two and a half bathrooms, and a small room which could be used as an office," Deborah said.

Instead of following Deborah, Hadley walked forward, pulling open the sliding glass door leading out onto the back porch. Bedrooms were one thing, but what she cared about most was what lay outside. Stepping out onto the large deck, Hadley smiled as a full, unobstructed view of the southern part of the valley opened in front of her. She could picture sitting in a nice comfortable chair, reading a book while glancing up to this beautiful scenery.

On top of the awesome view, the backyard also had a mature garden with beds running down both sides and a few fruit trees in the middle. There looked to be peas, lettuce, purple cabbages, strawberries, and tomatoes. Hadley even noticed a few beehives near the back corner, next to a covered stack of firewood.

Hadley turned as Deborah and Luke walked out onto the deck after her. "It's amazing. Are you sure it's in my price range?"

Deborah nodded. "Near the top, but yes. I figured this would be one you'd be willing to stretch for."

Luke asked, "And no one else knows about the place yet?"

"Not yet," Deborah said. "But you know how this town works."

He clicked his tongue. "That's what I was worried about." He turned to Hadley. "If you're already going to be stretching to give him his asking price, I don't know if it's going to be enough."

Hadley's forehead wrinkled in confusion. "Why wouldn't it be enough?"

"Because I think you're going to be in a bidding war for this place and asking is only where that will start."

"Why will I be in a bidding war when no one else knows?" Hadley put a hand on her hip.

Luke crossed his arms over his chest. "Because I want this place too."

❧ 18 ❧

Hadley was sure she was going to have to pay someone to refinish the wood floors in her living room from all of the pacing she'd done upon returning home after seeing Leo's house.

Or maybe she should save her money for the dental work she was going to need to fix the teeth she would likely crack if she continued to grit them like she'd been doing ever since Luke announced he was going to bid for the house too.

She picked up Marmalade—sure she was keeping her now, she'd named her after the citrus preserve and its orange color. Petting the kitten's soft fur, Hadley to try to calm herself.

"That man is the most infuriating ... jerk I've ever met," she grumbled to herself as she continued to pace.

"You wouldn't be talking about me, now, would you, Had?"

Hadley jumped and spun around to see Tyler standing in the doorway to the kitchen. He raised one dark eyebrow as he leaned into the doorframe. He was wearing the same bluish-black jeans as yesterday, it seemed, but he'd changed into a red T-shirt featuring some Seattle brewery's logo on the front. An odd mixture of annoyance and nostalgia washed over Hadley. Red had always been her favorite color on Tyler.

Marmalade stiffened at the sight of him, however, and jumped out of Hadley's arms, skittering off to join Ansel on the couch.

Tyler peered over at them. "Two cats? We've been divorced less than a year, and you're already becoming a crazy cat lady." He laughed.

She didn't.

"What are you doing, Ty? You don't live here anymore. You can't just waltz in whenever you want."

He put his hands up in defense. "I came to help. You said it would be nice if I did."

Exhaling, Hadley said, "Okay, but next time would you at least knock?"

Tyler agreed, and she showed him to the spare bedroom, where she'd stored all of the things she needed his opinion on.

In only half an hour, they'd gone through all the books in their library and half of the photo albums, splitting things up as evenly as they could. Tyler had begun a pile of things he would bring with him when he went back over the mountains. There was a donation pile, and Hadley brought a box over to pack the things she was going to keep.

She balked as she picked up their wedding album. Her gaze tiptoed up to meet his.

Tyler caught sight of what she held and cleared his throat. "Oh, wow." But instead of sitting in the discomfort like she was, he took it from her and plopped into the chair in the corner of the room. Flipping open the cover, a wide smile overtook his face. "Man, look at these kids."

Enticed, Hadley walked over and perched on the arm of the chair, leaning in to see the nineteen-year-old versions of them. His hair was longer and shaggier, while hers was shorter, curled into soft waves hanging around her shoulders. Tyler had bulked up since then, though not necessarily in a bad way. Hadley brushed a hand along her hip, knowing she'd gained some weight in that area. But other than being skinnier and a decade younger, the people in the photo also had an innocence to them which made Hadley want to cry.

"They look so happy," Tyler said.

"They had no idea what was coming, did they?" she added.

Sadness washed over Tyler's features as he glanced up at her. After she'd found out about what he'd actually been doing when he said he was going on all of his business trips, he'd said he was sorry so many times Hadley lost count. And while his apologies made it easier to be in the same room with him, they couldn't erase her distrust.

Letting go of one side of the album, Tyler reached over and took her hand with his. He moved like he wanted to pull her into his lap like he used to, but he hesitated and must've rethought that because he just squeezed her hand, instead.

"What should we do with this?" Tyler asked, finally.

Hadley let go of his hand and moved back over to the pile of albums. She moved two and then pulled out a black leather one. "We have two. This is the one the photographer made us." She pointed to the album still in his hands. "That's the one your mom put together. You keep that one, and I'll take this."

He nodded, then continued to flip through the pages of the one he held.

"Ty," she whispered. When he looked up, she said, "We've got a lot to go through. As much as I'd like to sit down and reminisce about how skinny my arms used to be, I don't think we have time."

She also didn't want to get caught looking through photos bound to make her feel sentimental and push her toward poor decisions.

Tyler seemed to understand. "Right." He cleared his throat and patted the album cover as he closed it.

Without two copies of the other albums in their collection, they had to employ a much more discretionary tactic for the rest of the pictures, but an hour later they'd finished.

"That wasn't so bad," Tyler said, standing and stretching.

Hadley patted off her pants since some of the pictures had been a little dusty and stood. "We haven't even started looking at furniture."

Tyler cringed in response, but as it turned out, neither of them needed to worry. They'd always butted heads when they'd been married, fighting over how to decorate the house, what kind of car to get, and even what to make for dinner. But now that they were no longer a couple, compromise felt so much easier. They went through the whole house, putting sticky notes on whatever they wanted.

"Your grandma gave us these," Hadley said, running her hand along the top of one of their matching bedside tables. "You should take them."

Running his hand along his chin, he nodded. "Okay, well then you get the headboard since your dad made that."

"Deal," she said.

"Deal." He held his hand out and she shook it.

Instead of letting go, however, he held on, holding her gaze with his just as intensely. She'd always had a soft spot for those brown eyes of his. Tyler tugged her closer to him until she could feel his breath on her neck.

She remembered what Deborah had said earlier about there always being a spark. She couldn't deny it. This was Tyler, after all. He was the first boy she'd dated and the one she'd spent so many years thinking was going to be her last.

"Had, I've missed you," he whispered as he bent closer, wrapping an arm around her waist.

Before Hadley could decide how she should react, what she should say, her phone began buzzing from where she'd tucked it in her back pocket. She pulled away from Tyler and took out the phone. It was Paul.

"Hey," she answered.

"You busy?" he asked.

Tyler stepped back, raking his fingers back and forth through his hair.

"No," she answered. "What's up?"

"I have a few questions for Barry. I think he'll take it better if you're there with me."

"Uh, sure." She had some questions of her own, but didn't want to ask them in front of Tyler.

"Be there in ten minutes."

Paul hung up before she could answer.

Tyler looked up. "That Paul?"

Hadley nodded.

"Then that's my cue to leave," he said, patting his pockets like he always did when he was making sure he had his keys and wallet. "If it's possible, that brother of yours has gotten bigger since the last time I was here, and I don't want to be on the receiving end of the knuckle sandwich I know he's dying to serve me."

Chuckling, Hadley couldn't argue.

Tyler walked past her and planted a kiss on her forehead

like he used to. Her chest tightened in pain as she watched him leave. They'd been working in the bedroom, and the spare bed was right in front of her, so she let herself fall, face-first into the comforter.

Ansel and Marmalade came trotting in after Tyler left. The sound of paws padding on the wood floor didn't even entice her to look up.

When Paul got there a few minutes later, Hadley was in the same spot. Ansel was curled up next to her head, and Marmalade had climbed onto her back and was perched there, purring away.

"Hey, you okay?" he asked.

The bed shifted as he sat on the edge.

"Mm ummfued."

"Come again?"

She lifted her face from the comforter and felt Marmalade jump off her back. "I'm confused."

"Would this confusion have anything to do with the fact that I passed Tyler on my way here?"

Hadley wrinkled her face into a frown. "Maybe."

He set a hand on her back and patted it a few times. "Sorry, Had. I know none of this can be easy."

"I can't tell if it would've been worse having to do all of this packing on my own, but gosh is it hard having him here again."

Paul shook his head. "I'm still in the *I wish he'd never show his face here again* camp, but that's just me."

Rolling onto her side, she asked, "So why do you need me to go talk to Barry with you? Did you guys hear back about the type of bee responsible for stinging Charlie?"

"Not yet, but we did find out what that sticky substance was on the handle."

Hadley sat up. "What?"

"Honey." Paul's forehead creased together as he watched her react.

"That's not good." Focusing on her fingers, Hadley began to pick the polish off one of her pink nails.

Paul sighed. "That's why I want to talk with him. I need to give him one last chance to come clean."

Hadley swallowed as a lump formed in her throat at the idea that Barry might've been responsible for Charlie's death. She got up off the bed.

"Well, I guess there's only one way to find out."

B arry's bee farm was only a few minutes away. Paul parked next to Barry's old red truck, and they headed for his house. It was an odd sensation for Hadley. Most of the times she'd visited the man, he'd been out working around the hives or on his garden. She'd been to Barry's house close to a hundred times in her life, but Hadley could count the times she'd gone inside on one hand.

Paul knocked on the faded front door. While Barry's house and farm were all mostly well maintained, they couldn't hide their age or the reality that one man was in charge of running the whole farm by himself.

When Barry opened the door moments later, he was just pulling on his normal newsboy-style cap.

"The James twins," he said with a hint of surprise. "To what do I owe this pleasure?" The old man's voice held a tremor that made Hadley quite sure he wasn't expecting the visit to be pleasurable.

Her stomach flipped. He knew why they were there, which meant he had done something to Charlie.

"Hey, Barry." Paul took off his sunglasses and stepped

inside. "I've got some questions for you." It didn't matter that Paul wasn't wearing his sheriff's uniform—Sundays being his usual day off each week—his tone, and the way he scanned the room made it clear they weren't just there for a social call.

"And your lovely sister is here to soften me up?" Barry asked. He set a hand on her arm, squeezing down through the slight shake in his fingers that seemed to have been present for the last ten years or so.

Hadley covered his hand with hers and patted it gently.

Paul tipped his head. "You know us too well, Barry."

"Come and sit, then." Barry motioned to the dining room table their father had made for him before they were born.

Hadley sat and let her finger trace over the beautiful knots in the dark wood.

"Can I get you anything to drink?" Barry asked, moving into the kitchen.

"I'll take a tea with honey, please," Hadley said. She wasn't thirsty, but she knew Barry loved to host guests and didn't get to do it as often as he liked.

"Same here, thank you." Paul sent Hadley a quick wink which was his way of telling her to relax.

In an effort to do so, she pushed her shoulders back and pulled in a deep breath. By the time she exhaled, Barry returned with a pot of honey.

He placed it on the table and said, "Kettle's on. So what do you wanna know?" He looked up from his cracked fingernails and let his gaze settle on Paul.

Paul's Adam's apple bobbed as he swallowed, probably buying himself one more moment. "Barry, this business with Charlie isn't looking great."

Barry's white mustache moved as he pressed his lips

together and nodded. Hadley felt like crying as she recognized the anguish sitting behind his eyes.

"If there's anything you can tell me that might shed some light on why you're all over the crime scene, I think it's time for you to come clean." Paul lifted his eyebrows, and though the gesture appeared intimidating, Hadley knew he was being much gentler than he normally would've been with a suspect.

The old man ran a hand over his beard. Just as he was about to say something, the whistle of the kettle stopped him. He held up a shaky finger and disappeared into the kitchen for a moment. He returned with a teapot and three stacking mugs.

"This needs to steep a bit," Barry explained as he set them down and then returned to his seat.

Hadley and Paul watched him.

Barry sighed. "By now I'm sure you know it was Charlie who was to blame for the loss of so many of my bees."

Paul nodded. Hadley held her breath.

"I think there was a moment when I very much wanted to hurt that man," Barry said, lowering his gaze to the table like a man ashamed. "It's possible if I was my younger self, I may have. But, no"—he shook his head—"I didn't kill Charlie."

Opening his mouth, Paul was about to say something when Barry held up his hand to stop him.

"However …" Barry added. "I did want to let him know his actions had consequences." Patting his chest, Barry pulled a folded piece of paper from the breast pocket in his flannel shirt. "I wrote him this note, threatening him to leave the market and Stoneybrook in general or else I would sue him for damages."

Unfolding the letter, the older man flattened it on the

table and pushed it closer to Paul and Hadley. Hadley scanned the handwritten text—letters which were simultaneously careful and precise, but also showed the slight wobble in his hand. Concentrating hard, Hadley tried not to let her lip curve up in appreciation as she read the man's *threat*. Between Barry's love of reading and his late wife's career in journalism, the warning was the most eloquently worded thing Hadley had read in a good while.

"But why do you still have this?" Paul asked. He pushed the note back toward Barry once he seemed sure Hadley had a chance to read it too.

Barry sighed. "I couldn't go through with it. I put it in his van, on the driver's seat, but I didn't even get back to my booth before I turned back and retrieved it." Barry tapped his temple. "Nina talks to me still, tells me what I'm doing wrong. And she did not like me leaving the note like that. Told me, *Barry, you talk to the man face-to-face or not at all*."

Hadley remembered Barry's wife, Nina. She was as kind as she was strict. The woman held everyone around her to the highest standards, but you couldn't be mad at her because she also held herself to the same expectations.

"Is that why you were acting so odd the morning Charlie died?" Hadley asked Barry.

He nodded. "I was shocked, first of all, but then I began to worry my fingerprints were going to be all over that van of his. When Paul didn't come knocking right away, I thought maybe someone else was at the top of your list, but then Hadley came sniffing around about the type of bees I kept, and I knew it was coming. I'm just sorry it took you coming here for me to come clean."

Barry reached over and began pouring tea into the mugs, handing one with a spoon to each of the James twins. He opened a jar of beautiful, amber honey. They each took a teaspoon and then Barry used his finger to clean up a drip on one side before recapping the jar.

Paul stared as Barry attempted to wipe the stickiness off his finger and onto a cloth napkin.

"Did you have honey on your fingers when you opened the van door?" Paul asked.

Barry looked down at his hands. "It's a good probability. I don't even notice it anymore. Nina used to complain that all of our door knobs were sticky as a child's fingers."

"But, I don't get it," Hadley said. "Where was Charlie when you were putting the note in his van and then taking it back out? He hadn't even set up a table at the market. No one had seen him yet." She turned to Paul. "If he wasn't in his van, where was he?"

Paul's eyebrows knit together as he took in Hadley's question. "You didn't see Charlie at all that morning?" Paul asked Barry.

Barry took a measured breath. "I thought I did, but I wasn't sure, so I didn't say anything."

"Where do you *think* you saw him?" Paul leaned closer, setting his tea down on the table.

"I didn't know the man well, so I couldn't be certain, but I thought he was across the street, talking to a woman."

Now it was Hadley's turn to lean forward. "What did the woman look like?"

"Smart dresser, even smarter car." Barry tipped his head to one side. "Shortish hair, shiny." He made a cutting motion next to his shoulder to show the length.

Hadley's eyes went wide. She cut a quick glance at Paul who nodded in agreement.

Vivian.

The James twins both took large gulps of their tea, finishing off the last bit and then stood.

"Thank you for talking to us, Barry," Paul said, holding out his hand. When Barry stood as well and took his hand to shake, Paul said, "Next time, please let us know this kind of thing first. Don't wait for me to come to you. If you're not guilty, there's nothing for you to worry about."

Barry tsked. "Sorry, Paul. Nina covered way too many stories about people being wrongfully accused and sentenced for me to believe it. Nothing against you, but until that bumbling sheriff is out of the picture, I'm going to err on the side of not going to jail if I can help it."

Hadley pressed her lips together to hide a smile.

Paul didn't look as amused. He clenched his jaw tight for a second before saying, "Before we go, it will speed up our ability to clear your name if we can take some pictures of your bees just to confirm their race?" Paul asked.

"Sure thing," Barry said. "I'm happy to help put the person responsible behind bars, just as long as it's not me."

Hadley and Paul followed him out to the field as he opened a few of the hives so Paul could snap a few pictures of the bees. Minutes later, when they were climbing into Paul's truck, Hadley shook her head.

"I know it means we still don't know who killed Charlie, but boy am I glad it wasn't Barry." She pushed her seat belt into the clip.

Paul didn't seem so excited, but Hadley knew he was still frustrated with the man from holding on to such important information. "At least we have another reason to talk to Vivian."

Hadley lifted her eyebrows. Maybe she shouldn't have canceled her appointment with the woman.

Watching her for a moment, Paul said, "You've been telling me it's Vivian this whole time. Why aren't you more excited about this?"

She shrugged. "I just can't help but wonder how Vivian would've gotten a hold of bees and when she would've had a chance to put them into the van if he was talking with her. Wouldn't Charlie have noticed that?"

"True. So you're thinking someone put the bees in the van after Barry was there, while Charlie was talking with Vivian?"

Hadley wracked her brain for anyone else who might have access to bees. Then it hit her. She hadn't thought much about it this morning because she'd been so interested in the house and the views, but now the beehive sitting in the corner of Leo's property stood out like a red, waving flag.

"Leo's selling the rental property," Hadley said.

Paul blinked, obviously unsure what it had to do with anything.

Hadley described how she and Luke had viewed it with Deborah that morning, and how it had a beehive on it.

"I'll get Kevin over there with a warrant tomorrow to see what kind of bees he's keeping." Paul started the truck and drove them back into town.

She nodded, but if she was honest with herself, Leo going to jail for the death of Charlie Lloyd wasn't much better than Barry.

❦ 20 ❧

Monday morning found Hadley walking under the purple-and-white-striped awning into Valley Wildflowers for her weekly arrangements. She was definitely not there to snoop about the case, nor had she any mind to say anything to Leo about her interest in his property. Asking him to pick her offer over Luke's would've been unethical ... right?

But it didn't matter anyway, because as she walked into the flower shop, Jessie appeared to be the only one there, again.

If anyone wanted Leo to go to jail *less* than Hadley, it had to be Jessie. Maybe she could help Hadley out, give her information that could exonerate her father, take him off the suspect list for good.

Jessie walked out from the back, balancing the three arrangements. She patted a rogue leaf off her shirt once she'd set them down.

"So I saw you're staying at the rental place on the river," Hadley said, trying to sound nonchalant.

"Yeah. It's great, isn't it?" Jessie said with a smile, but it quickly faded. "Oh, no. I didn't leave a mess, did I? Please don't tell my dad. He told me I had to keep it nice if I was going to stay there."

Holding up her hands, Hadley shook her head. "Whoa. No, nothing like that. I saw a bag, and Deborah told me it was yours. The place looked great."

Jessie visibly relaxed. "Good. I really don't want to do anything to stress Dad out right now. I know he really needs to sell the rental. He's under a lot of pressure right now. I don't want to make it worse."

Seeing her opening, Hadley said, "Of course. I know what it's like to be under financial strain, to not know how tomorrow's going to turn out. That plus this whole Charlie deal, and he's got to be stressed to the max."

Jessie nodded along with Hadley's statement until she reached the part about Charlie. At the mention of Leo's dead competition, Jessie's eyes narrowed. "He didn't kill him; you know that, Hadley." Her sharp tone was quite a change from the sweet, lilting one she'd used on the phone.

"I want to believe it, Jess, but it's not looking good. If you have any information that can help take the spotlight off him, please let me know. Until then, Paul's not doing his job if he doesn't look into your dad."

Her face pinched together, tight. For a moment, it seemed like she was going to tell Hadley to leave, but then her features relaxed. "I was running an errand for him in the city, so I wasn't here. Hadley, I don't have anything to tell you to take suspicion off him except that I'm sure he didn't do it."

Hadley sighed. "Okay, what about Charlie? Do you know anything about him that might point us to someone else who hated him enough to want him dead?"

"I don't know anything other than how much of a jerk

he was to my dad and what a creep he was to me," Jessie said, then softened as she must've realized it wasn't helping her case. "His assistant manager, Stuart, would know more. That guy has been right beside Charlie for as long as I can remember."

"Right. I met him." Hadley nodded. "You know, he seemed pretty disgruntled. Do you think he could've done it?" Hadley remembered Paul had interrupted her the first time she'd tried to talk to the young man. Maybe he warranted another visit.

Just as she was starting to build a possible scenario in her mind where Stuart was the killer, Jessie shook her head. "I mean, I would've thought that too. The guy's a complete jerk, even worse than his boss. But I ran into him on my errand. We both go to the same supply warehouse on the other side of the mountains. We just buy supplies for our arrangements whereas they often buy bulk flowers." Jessie shrugged. "That doesn't matter anymore. What is important is he was there at the warehouse the same time I was. I remember because we glared at each other the whole time we were shopping. I didn't get home until well after noon, which means Stuart couldn't have been here much before that either."

Hadley chewed on her lip as she thought. She picked at her fingernails, but it appeared all of the polish she'd painted on the other day was already gone. This had been a stressful two weeks, it seemed.

"Okay. Thanks, Jessie." Hadley balanced the arrangements in her arms. "Maybe I'll see if I can go talk with Stuart. See if he knows anything."

Jessie waved goodbye as Hadley left. It wasn't until she was halfway down the street she remembered she was going to try to put in a good word about her offer on the house. *Oh well*, she thought. *Catching a killer is more important than me getting my dream house.* There would be time to talk about the house once this whole murder investigation was behind them.

Unless Luke put in an offer she couldn't beat, of course. Hadley shook her head. She couldn't think about Luke anymore, or she was going to have to wear a mouth guard to protect her teeth from all the grinding.

❧

Hadley spent the whole day on Monday in her kitchen making jam. She hadn't realized it, but between packing, running around looking at houses, and investigating Charlie's murder, she needed a full day alone in her kitchen.

There was something inherently calming to her about being surrounded by the sugary, tart smell of the jam as she cooked it and transferred it into the jars. Not to mention it was predictable. All Hadley had to do was follow her recipe and everything would turn out sweet and wonderful. She needed those kinds of results after weeks of nothing going as planned, it seemed.

Her bike ride home was lovely. Sunset was a few hours off still, but low clouds were blocking the hottest of the sun's rays, and it sounded as if the crickets were rejoicing in the reprieve after a heat-soaked day. Their chirps rose up from the fields and mixed with the tonal melodies of songbirds and the rhythmic rushing of sprinklers. The peace of nature felt as if it had fully enveloped her by the time she reached her road.

But it all fell away as she noticed Tyler's car sitting in the driveway.

To be honest, their divorce was still fresh enough she

hadn't registered his car's presence as wrong at first. Seeing Tyler's sporty, black sedan in that spot had been common-place since the year before when he'd bought it to get better gas mileage for all of the trips he had to make over the mountains for work.

Right. *Work*.

At the reminder, Hadley's face grew red. Not with anger, but embarrassment. She'd almost kissed the man the other day, had let him pull her close and tell her he missed her as if he hadn't been the one to push her away in the first place.

Hadley skidded her bike to a stop a few hundred feet back, wondering if she should go to Suze's instead and wait until he left. Maybe she couldn't be trusted around Tyler.

It was in times like these she wished her parents were here. Sure, Hadley was a thirty-year-old woman with a successful business. But sometimes she just needed her mom to brush her hair back out of her face and tell her how strong she was, and she needed her dad to call her "buddy" and remind her any boy who dared hurt her would have to answer to him.

Just thinking about them made her feel stronger, though, and Hadley pedaled the remaining distance to the house, determined to stand up to Tyler just as strongly as she had the day she'd told him she wanted a divorce.

He was sitting on the porch steps squinting at his phone when she came to a stop just outside the fence. Stepping off the bike and unclipping her helmet, Hadley wheeled the bike down the small hill and propped it up against the side of the house so it was protected under the eaves.

"You would fit right in with Seattleites," he said when she walked up. "They bike everywhere. A lot of people don't even have cars if they live downtown."

Hadley held the chin strap of her helmet, tight. The

reason she still rode a bike was in part because of all of their money he'd thrown at his affair. It was the same reason her jam kitchen still had a sign in the window saying, "Retail Space Opening Soon." While she wanted to renovate the front part of the kitchen into a small shop, she just didn't have the funds to do so after he'd depleted their savings.

But yelling at Tyler about all of that wasn't going to make her feel any better. Instead she released her grip on her helmet and said, "What's up?"

"We didn't quite finish yesterday." He stood, putting his phone away in his back pocket. Stepping toward her, Tyler placed a hand on her arm. "I thought we could pick up where we left off."

From the twinkle in his eye and the soft tone he was using, there was little doubt in Hadley's mind that he was talking about something other than packing.

And even though her heart beat so fast and hard in her chest she thought it might break free, she pulled in a deep breath and shook her head. She placed her hand over his. Instead of holding on to it—like he must've expected with the way his eyes lit up—Hadley moved his hand off her arm.

"Ty," she said, sighing. "We're over. You made that very clear. You can't come back here and play house with me just because you're feeling sentimental and homesick, or whatever's going on here."

His handsome face fell. That was one thing Hadley had learned growing up with Tyler Henley; the man was not used to hearing the word no. He was also one of the most stubborn people she'd ever met.

Taking her hands in his again, Tyler said, "You've got to admit there's still something here, Had. We've been together almost half our lives. I don't know how to be without you."

She cocked an eyebrow. "You didn't seem to have a problem being without me when you were sleeping with Christina all of those months."

He dropped her hands to run one of his through his hair. "I was having a … quarter-life crisis, or whatever they're calling them now."

It was hard to see him like this. She was too used to the smooth, popular quarterback whose smile could light up any room and who was always the life of the party. Now, before her, stood a broken man. A man who'd broken himself.

"We can work through this, Had," he said, worry taking control of his once even tone.

The statement made Hadley blink. Of course they could. That had never been the problem, she realized. The problem had always been that neither of them was truly happy, truly who they should be when they were together. Besides regular marital bickering here and there, they didn't have any huge problems that would've pushed him into Christina's arms. If anyone would've asked Hadley how they were doing up until the moment she'd gotten the email from his mistress, she would've told them they were *great, happy, the best.*

Deborah may have been right the other day when she'd said there would always be a spark. He would always be part of her life, but it didn't mean he deserved to be her whole life anymore.

"I'm sorry, Ty. I can't."

Hadley placed her hands on either side of his face and leaned up. She kissed him on the cheek, squeezing back the tears threatening to break free from where they stung in the corners of her eyes.

When she pulled back, a scraping sound rang out from behind her. Tyler's gaze flicked up toward the road.

Luke Fenton stood up at the end of the driveway. He wore the worn, red baseball cap he'd had since high school. He'd rolled the sleeves of his work shirt up revealing his tanned arms. And he was on foot. Had he walked all the way there?

"Luke?" Hadley called out, but it was too late.

He'd waved, pulled off his cap, and headed in the other direction before she or Tyler could say anything more.

Tyler scuffed the toe of his shoes on the stepping stones. "I guess I should go and see what Luke wanted from me."

"I think that would be best." Hadley wrapped her arms around her middle and watched him leave.

That night while Hadley was going through her kitchen cabinets and packing anything nonessential, Paul called. He started the conversation with the last subject Hadley wanted to discuss at that moment.

"How's the house hunt going?"

She groaned. "Frustrating." She was too tired to elaborate much more than that and didn't want to explain how Luke Fenton was going to get her dream house instead of her.

Paul was silent for a moment, as if he was waiting for her to say something else. When she didn't, he said, "Okay … well, I have some news that might cheer you up."

"What?" She used the kitchen counter to help her get up off the floor.

"We got news about the bees. Barry's are Italian, just like he told you."

"And the ones that killed Charlie?"

"Russian."

Relief escaped Hadley through a long sigh. "Oh, good. So are you removing him from your suspect list?"

159

"Not officially since he doesn't have a concrete alibi, but McKay's focusing elsewhere.

"That's great news. So why does your voice have mad-Paul written all over it?"

He took a measured breath. "He's now convinced Leo's the killer."

Hadley cringed, having had a feeling that was coming. "And what do you think?"

Even though her brother was often as blinded by his love of their town and its inhabitants as she was, Hadley knew he'd been trying to work on putting the law before his feelings.

"I know the evidence doesn't look good against Leo, but there's still not enough to convict him, thankfully. Until that point, I'm not going to jump to any conclusions."

Hadley smiled, glad her brother was more discerning than the ornery sheriff he worked for and also glad the law prevented them from jumping to too many conclusions about suspects.

"So where do you go from here?" she asked. "If we're hoping Leo's innocent and Barry's not the killer, you're down to Vivian?"

"I guess. There's still the fact that her husband's alibi is unsubstantiated. He could've done this if he found out about the affair. He didn't seem to know who Charlie was, but people lie."

"Or he and Vivian could've been working together to get rid of him."

"Right. Regardless, I want to go up to Cascade Ridge tomorrow and ask the two of them a few more questions. You busy?"

Hadley chewed on her bottom lip. She'd gotten a lot more done today than she'd planned, so she was in an okay spot jam-wise. Packing-wise, she felt nowhere near done, but going investigating sounded so much more interesting.

"I could go with you, but are you sure you want me to? Vivian knows you're a deputy, and my cover will be blown. Not that I was able to find out a ton from her, other than I don't want to move to Cascade Ridge, but I figure we want to keep her thinking I'm a potential buyer just in case I need to set up another appointment."

"I thought about that too. I don't want you to come with me when I talk to Vivian. I was thinking we could split up. You can talk with Stuart while I question Vivian. I know you mentioned Jessie told you Charlie's assistant manager would be the one to ask about anyone else wanting Charlie dead. I want to make sure we're not overlooking any other possibilities."

Hadley could tell by the tightness in Paul's voice that what he was telling her wasn't the whole truth.

"Stuart won't talk with you, will he?"

Paul cleared his throat. "He was less than cooperative the other day when I tried to question him. He seemed to like you and Suze, though."

"Amazing what the lack of a uniform will get you," she observed, chuckling. "And, yes, I'll do it."

"Thanks, Had. I'll pick you up at eight."

"Got it. Night."

Hadley held the phone for a moment, lost in thought, before setting it down. She glanced over at the bundle of sleeping cats on the back of the couch and smiled.

"Good idea, you two. I'd better get some sleep if I'm going to get to the bottom of this case tomorrow."

And sleep she did, like a rock. So much so she must've slept right through her alarm.

"Had. Wake up."

She fluttered her eyes open to see Paul standing over her.

"Omigosh!" She bolted upright. "I'm so sorry, I—" Flipping the covers over, she jumped out of bed and scooted into her bathroom. Before closing the door behind her, she poked her head back out, catching sight of the still-stunned Paul. "I'll be two seconds. Promise."

Two seconds was, of course, a gross underestimate, but she was ready to go in less than ten minutes.

By the time she'd emerged from her bathroom, Paul must've gone downstairs to wait because her bedroom was empty, except for the cats still lounging on her bed. She jogged down the stairs and stuck her landing after jumping over the last two. Paul laughed as she threw up her arms like a gymnast, punctuating her *almost* timely arrival.

She let her arms drop. "Sorry. I don't know the last time I overslept like that."

"You've been a little stressed out lately. It's okay." He threw an arm across her shoulders and ruffled her just-brushed hair. "Let's get going, oversleeper. There's a coffee and scone waiting for you in my truck."

Hadley sighed and grabbed her purse. "I knew you were my favorite brother for a reason."

The drive up to Cascade Ridge was consumed with talk of their strategies as they prepared for their different lines of questioning. Paul was going to get a straight answer out of Vivian about what she'd been doing in Stoneybrook that morning since they now had an eyewitness who'd seen Charlie talking to her right before he died. Hadley was bent on finding out if there were any suspects they may be missing by talking to Stuart. She was hoping Jessie had been right when she'd said he was the one to know Charlie best.

"Good luck. Call if you need anything," Paul said as he dropped her off a block away from Bloom.

Hadley gave him a nod then closed the door. She ran a hand through her sleep-crumpled locks and hoped the five minutes she took to get ready wouldn't make her appear disheveled or untrustworthy.

Pulling open the glass front door, Hadley eyed the **Under New Management** sign hanging in the window. *That's interesting*, she thought as she entered.

"Welcome to Bloom," a voice called from somewhere Hadley couldn't place.

She whirled around, looking for the person.

"Oh, over here," Stuart said, standing up from where he'd been kneeling behind the counter. "Sorry, I had a bit of a change explosion when I was filling the register."

Hadley waved a hand in his direction. "No worries. I'm glad to see you're still here. I was worried you might've been out of a job when I saw the sign in the window."

The young man pointed to his name tag, a big smile pulling across his face. "Kind of the opposite, actually."

Taking a few steps closer, Hadley read the new *Manager* title under his name. "Wow, congrats. So he left the place to you, then?"

Stuart shook his head. "He left it to his sister, but she lives in California and had no interest in it. I convinced her to give me a year to prove I could run the place. She'll remain a silent owner, and I'll show her I can make it worth her while."

"That's amazing. Very ambitious for someone your age. What are you, eighteen?"

"Twenty," he said flatly. His demeanor brightened back up as he added, "And I was already in school double majoring in horticulture and business."

Hadley's eyebrows rose. "A double major. Good for you."

He dipped his chin. "Yeah, it's intense, but I'm taking classes this summer to make sure I can fit everything in." He sighed. "So what can I help you with?" he asked. "You and your friend left so quickly when that deputy came in. You in trouble with the law or something like that?"

"Something like that." Hadley cringed. It was one of the few times she was glad she and Paul didn't look like twins. Stuart hadn't caught on that she and Paul were at all related. "Sorry it took me so long to get back here."

An idea struck Hadley, and she ran with it.

"I've been crazy busy with trying to buy a house. I'm kinda on a deadline as the place I'm currently in closes in a couple weeks, and I still haven't found anywhere new." She picked at the polish she'd managed to put on her nails last night. "I'm working with Vanderberg Realty, but I'm not quite sure if it's the right fit. Do you know anything about them?"

Stuart's face darkened. "Which realtor?"

"Vivian Harris." She watched him as her answer hit.

He shook his head. "I mean, the woman's good at her job, but it's your funeral."

Hadley leaned forward. "Why's that?"

Stuart's cheeks reddened. "Sorry, you're probably fine using her to buy a house. I would just be careful getting any closer, if I were you."

"Because?" Hadley asked, noticing he still hadn't answered her question.

Stuart stared at her for an uncomfortable moment. Then, when she thought he was just about to tell her not to worry about it, he said, "Because I'm pretty sure she's the reason my boss is dead."

Hadley hadn't expected him to come right out and say it like that. "Seriously?" She tried to feign ignorance, to pretend she didn't also believe the same thing.

Stuart glanced behind her at the door to the shop, then he said, "Charlie and Vivian were having an affair. He broke it off about a week ago. She told him she was going to stop using Bloom for staging like Vanderberg Realty often did, so he threatened to tell her husband. The man showed up dead a few days later. Coincidences like that just don't happen."

"Wow. That—" Hadley went to shake her head, but she stopped. "How do you know they were having an affair?" It wasn't new information to her, but she wanted to hear what Stuart knew.

The young man let out a humorless laugh. "I know everything about Charlie." His eyes flicked down to his hands. "Well … knew."

Hadley put a hand on her hip.

"I'm serious. You don't work as the sole employee for a man for four years and not get to know him. Plus, Charlie ran his mouth, a lot. I knew exactly how his divorce from his wife went down three years ago. I knew what size and brand of jeans he wore. I knew where he got his hair cut and how often. I knew anything spicy would give the man terrible heartburn for two days after. I knew he was extremely allergic to bee stings." Stuart pulled out a drawer next to him and pointed to two EpiPens stored near the front. He winced and then closed the drawer. "Well … I suppose everyone kinda knows that now."

"Right." Hadley swallowed down heat that crept up her throat at the memory of seeing Charlie dead in his flower van. "If he was so allergic, why didn't he keep one of those with him?" Hadley asked, pointing to the drawer of life-saving medicine.

Stuart's face morphed into a frown. "That's what I can't figure out. He keeps one in the glovebox in the van. I'm not sure why he didn't use it."

Hadley remembered Paul saying they'd searched the whole van and found nothing of the sort.

"Do you think someone hid it?" she asked.

"It's possible. Like I said, Charlie ran his mouth. I think half of his customers knew about the allergy. He would even take out the pens every once in a while to demonstrate how he would have to slam the needle into his thigh if anything were ever to happen. I wouldn't be surprised if half the city knows where he kept all of those pens."

Hadley chewed on her bottom lip as she thought. "Do you have any idea if Vivian has access to bees?"

Stuart scratched his chin. "That's the one thing that doesn't make sense to me. Though, I suppose you can get anything you want on the internet these days." He shrugged.

"True." Hadley pressed her lips together as she thought. "And you're sure there's no one else who would've had motive to kill Charlie?"

Stuart shook his head. He looked around the shop, obviously tiring of her questions.

"I suppose I should get those flowers this time." Hadley smiled. "I'll take these two bouquets." She pointed to a particularly beautiful matching set complete with lavender, roses, and even a few sage-green succulents.

"Good choice," Stuart beamed. "Those are some new designs I'm trying out. Charlie would have never let me get away with something this contemporary."

Hadley tipped her head as she studied the arrangement. She pointed to a particularly purple cluster of jade. "You know, this is just like something Leo from Valley Wildflowers down in Stoneybrook might make." After she'd already said it, Hadley wished she could take the compliment back, remembering about their rivalry and how Stuart would probably see it as more of a put-down than anything else. "Sorry. I didn't mean—"

He put up a hand to stop her.

"Thanks. I know he and Charlie had their ups and downs, but I'm hoping to cut a new path with the local shops, especially that one."

Hadley nodded. "That's a great idea." She held her tongue about the disparaging things she'd heard Jessie spout about Stuart the other day, hoping the young man would be able to change her mind.

"Though it might be hard to do. Last time Leo and his daughter ran into Charlie, the man just about assaulted her," Stuart added.

What if Leo saw Charlie hitting on his nineteen-year-old daughter and decided that was the last straw?

"Oh, that's awful." Hadley cringed.

Stuart tipped his head to the side. "Hey," he said. "You know him, then?"

She clenched her teeth, realizing she needed to be more careful about what she said. Unsure whether or not admitting to knowing Leo would blow her cover story, Hadley nodded. "Um, yeah."

"Do you think you could … you know, put in a good word for me?" He dug around in his pocket, finally pulling out a woman's hair tie, two bobby pins, and a tampon.

Stuart glanced up at her, embarrassment coloring his cheeks pink.

"Sorry. My girlfriend is always asking me to hold stuff like this. She's on this whole small-purse kick, so my pockets and my car just seem to take over everything that won't fit anymore." He shoved the handful of stuff back and dug into his other pocket, producing a worn business card.

Hadley smiled as he held it out to her. "No problem," she said. "I'd be happy to let him know you're looking to turn over a new leaf." She laughed and flicked her fingers at a leaf in the bouquet to accent her pun.

He must've been grateful to her, because Stuart laughed entirely too loud at her joke. "Thanks. I really appreciate it."

Stuart rang her up for the bouquets and waved as she headed outside. Glancing down at her phone through the leaves and petals of the arrangements, Hadley read a text from Paul.

Meet you in the same spot in ten?

She sent a thumbs-up text back and walked in the direction of where he'd dropped her off, hoping her brother had gotten what he needed on Vivian.

❦ 2 2 ❦

Paul pulled up to the curb at their meeting spot just moments after Hadley arrived on foot. Once inside the car, she buckled in and positioned the bouquets in her lap, making sure she could still see Paul. Turning to watch her brother, she tried to read his expression. The way his dark eyebrows were pulled low and tight, casting a shadow over his eyes.

"Oh no. What's wrong?" Hadley asked, recognizing the frustration in his features.

Paul pulled out into traffic, but kept facing forward.

"Vivian wouldn't talk?"

"She didn't need to. I got a call from McKay and went to the station instead."

Leaning closer, Hadley felt her heartbeat rise in anticipation.

Paul glanced over at her. "You're not going to like it."

Hadley felt her face pull into a similar scowl as the one her brother was still sporting.

"Vivian's cleared."

"She's what?"

"There's no surveillance in the lot at Fenton Park, but once I convinced McKay Vivian was a viable suspect, he had me go around collecting any and all footage from southern Main Street. Well, I mean, it was basically the grocery store and Louise in the knitting shop who had any cameras. The guys at the station looked through for evidence and Louise's camera managed to catch Vivian pulling up, getting out, fighting with Charlie, and then getting back into her car until Suze approached and she split. Charlie came to her, so she was never out of view of the camera. She didn't kill Charlie."

As she processed the information, Hadley kept opening her mouth, thinking she had something to say, but then she would change her mind and snap it shut again. She felt like a fish after the third time, so she pressed her lips together.

Paul sighed. "Which means we're back at square Leo. Unless you learned something from the kid just now."

She scrunched her forehead. Stuart hadn't told her anything she didn't already know—well, other than accusing an innocent person, apparently.

Finding her voice, Hadley said, "Nope. Nothing. Looks like Leo's the only square left." She squinted. "Except Vivian's husband."

Paul shook his head. "McKay questioned him. He's adamant he didn't have any idea about Charlie and denied his wife being involved with anyone else."

Slumping back into her seat, Hadley said, "What happens next, then?"

"McKay is filing for an arrest warrant right now. It'll probably take a day or so, and then he'll go pick up Leo. With the warrant, we can search his house and shop."

The scenery flew by as Paul took the winding forest road away from Cascade Ridge and into the valley. Hadley didn't know what to say. She didn't know what to do anymore. When there were multiple suspects, she was able to convince herself it wasn't the local florist. But now …

Frustrated, she focused on the beautiful flowers in her lap. Flowers were uncomplicated, just wonderfully colorful and fragrant. She leaned forward and smelled a particularly gorgeous rose. One of the lavender fronds tickled her nose in the process. She let out a huge sneeze.

"Bless you," Paul said.

She sneezed again.

He chuckled.

And again. "Oooff." She groaned, holding her hand up to her nose.

"There are tissues in the glovebox," he said, keeping his eyes on the road.

Jostling the flowers so they were in between the two of them, Hadley opened the compartment in front of her, grabbing a tissue from the box inside. But before she could pull her hand out and close the glovebox, she noticed something else inside.

One of Suze's painted hair sticks.

Hadley blinked at it for a moment, brain seeming to slog through the reality of what it meant. *Since when did Suze ride in Paul's car enough to warrant leaving hair sticks in here?* They were all over her house and art studio, but she didn't even leave them in the Jam Van, and she rode in that all the time with Hadley. That meant Suze had spent a considerable amount of time in Paul's car …

The image of Stuart emptying out a handful of his girlfriend's stuff from his pockets came to mind.

Pulling her hand back, her eyes shot over to Paul to see if he'd noticed what she'd found, but he was still looking ahead.

Omigosh, omigosh, omigosh! Paul and Suze? Paul and Suze!

Hadley's thoughts bounced erratically between elation and disbelief. She'd wanted this to happen for so long. Their odd behavior over the past few weeks *had* been a sign that something was going on. She knew they were keeping someth—

Wait. They'd been keeping it from her. Why?

She slammed the glovebox closed, suddenly feeling awkward as if she'd walked in on a secret.

"Whoa," Paul said. "Easy there. This is my favorite truck, you know?"

"Sorry." Hadley knew her voice was tight and awkward.

He glanced over at her. "Everything okay?"

"Sure. Everything okay with *you*?" She watched him closely. "With this case taking up all of your time, we haven't been able to chat much. Is there anything you need to *chat* about?"

Paul chuckled at her, obviously mistaking her discomfort for silliness. "I'm not the one whose ex came back to town recently. Is there anything *you* need to *chat* about?" he asked, turning her questions back on her.

Avoidance. Why would he keep this from her?

Dejected, she let herself sink back into the seat. "I'm fine."

"Yeah, you sound super great." He shook his head. "Well, you know where to find me when you're ready to talk."

He elbowed her playfully, but it just made Hadley want to cry. She looked out the window. The twins rode the rest of the way back into Stoneybrook in silence.

"Can you drop me at the kitchen?" she asked as soon as downtown came into view.

"But you don't have your bike with you. How will you get home?" he asked, coming to a stop next to her lavender-and-white awning.

"I'll walk. I think it sounds nice today." She kissed her hand and planted it on his cheek then gathered her flowers from the back before he had a chance to argue. "Thanks for letting me come along."

Paul waved as he pulled away. She pushed her shoulders back. "Time to let this case go. The law has it under control, and I've got enough to worry about."

Hadley decided, in one exhaled breath, it was past time to call Deborah and put in an offer on Leo's house. She'd been holding off, trying to figure out if there was anywhere else she could find more money to add to her bid. But a day's worth of thinking and she was still coming up empty. She would just have to make the offer she could, hope Luke's wasn't too much higher than hers, and leave it up to Leo.

If he wasn't already in jail.

Her stomach churned at the thought. Shaking her head, she went inside the jam kitchen, pulling out her phone. Deborah picked up on the second ring.

"Hadley, I was going to call you today if I didn't hear from you. I was surprised I didn't hear from you right after I showed you the house." She chuckled.

"Yeah, sorry. I was trying to think of any way I might be able to up my offer."

"Oh, because Luke's interested? I'm so sorry about that. I had no idea he would want that place at all since it doesn't meet half of his look-fors. I feel terrible."

Hadley said, "Don't worry about it. I just don't know

how I'll be able to compete with him. He's got to have a substantial downpayment with that company of his getting so big."

"I would expect nothing less." Deborah sighed. "I told him I wouldn't represent him, that he'd have to find someone else to put his bid in since I had specifically showed the property to you. I wouldn't feel right otherwise."

"Thanks, Deborah."

"That doesn't mean he won't be able to find someone else. Though, I will say he hasn't put an offer in yet, so that's hopeful."

Hadley ran her thumbnail across the surface of her nails even though there wasn't a hint of polish left to chip off. "I guess. Or he's just waiting until the last second."

"Right …"

They sat in silence for a moment.

Deborah broke it, saying, "Well, let me know when you want to come in, and I'll write up an offer for you to sign."

She listed a few times that worked for her. Hadley made an appointment to drop by that afternoon. Before Hadley could put her phone away after the call with Deborah, a text from Suze came through. It was just a coffee cup emoji. She bit her lip and sent back a thumbs-up. Maybe Paul wouldn't talk to her about them but Suze would come clean. Right?

Moments later, she was waiting in front of the jam kitchen, basking in the shade of one of the maple trees dotted along Main Street. Suze came walking toward her, a conspiratorial glint in her eye.

"What's that for?" Hadley asked, hope rising in her heart. She'd been right. Suze couldn't keep something this big from her.

Suze smiled and said, "I know something you don't know."

Hadley stiffened. "Are you sure?"

Arching an eyebrow, Suze cocked her head. "Pretty sure."

"Does it have to do with Paul?"

Suze shook her head. "No, not the case." She grabbed Hadley's arm. "Oh, unless … did you find out who did it yet?"

"Actually, we're further away from finding the killer than ever, it feels." She sighed.

As they walked to the coffee shop, Hadley filled Suze in on Paul taking her to Cascade Ridge with him, and how Vivian had been taken off the suspect list after the video footage had come through.

"Darn. So we're back to Leo?" she asked as they pulled open the creaky wooden door to the coffee shop.

Hadley nodded sadly, then remembered that Suze was about to tell her a secret. "Wait … What were you going to tell me earlier? What was the secret?"

Suze's mouth hung open, and she looked forward in line. "Uh, well actually …" She pointed discreetly behind Hadley. "That's it."

Hadley turned around and spotted Tyler standing at the front of the line, ordering a coffee. She was about to remind Suze she'd already seen Tyler and that he wasn't a secret when the man finished ordering and turned around to wait on the other end of the counter.

His whole cheek was red, swollen, and a bruise was beginning to spread upward toward his left eye. He also had a pretty nasty cut on his lip.

He noticed Hadley through his slightly squinted vision, and his face softened. She raced forward as he dipped his head and took a step toward her. They met in the middle.

"What happened?" she asked, ignoring the fact that

people were staring. It looked as if most of the people inside the coffee shop were tourists, not locals.

Tyler's tongue wet his lips, stopping at the cut along the right corner. He winced. "Nothing I wouldn't repeat to stick up for you."

"Me?" Hadley's cheeks heated up as she realized how loudly she'd said that. Quieter, she asked. "What do I have to do with this?" She gestured to his face as she felt Suze sidle up next to her.

"It was crazy." Tyler shook his head. "I was talking to Luke when he mentioned the two of you were interested in the same property. I told him he needed to back off and let you have it. Out of the blue, the man went crazy and punched me." Tyler mimed a quick left, right combination of punches. "He stomped off. I haven't seen him since." Hadley's ex shrugged.

She glanced over at Suze to confirm that this was the story she'd heard. Suze nodded.

So it wasn't about her and Paul at all.

"That doesn't make any sense." Hadley wrinkled her brow. "Why would Luke attack you?"

Tyler scoffed. "He's been acting weird as all get out for about a year now. I feel like I don't even know the man anymore."

Just the opposite of my experience, Hadley thought, feeling like she'd only just started to recognize the boy she'd grown up with, in the past few months. Nails free of polish, Hadley picked at her cuticles as she thought.

Tyler's hand settled on her arm. She looked up to meet the serious gaze he had trained on her.

"I hope you know I would do anything for you, Had." He winked at her with his non-swollen eye.

Hadley pressed her lips together. When she'd first found out about the truth behind all of Tyler's "business trips," she'd spent a long time reflecting on why she hadn't caught on. It was then that she fully realized she couldn't read him like she could the other people in her life.

No, the problem wasn't her inability to tell if he was lying, it was the fact that maybe he always was lying—had been for a long time.

So when he told her he would do anything for her, no swooning ensued. In fact, she was more likely to add to the scratches on his face than she was to fall into his arms. But she also didn't want to cause a scene.

She closed her eyes. "I'm sorry you two got in a fight. It wasn't necessary for you to stand up for me. I can do it for myself." When her lids fluttered back open, Tyler was looking down at her, disapprovingly.

"Tyler, your Americano is ready," Wendy called from behind the counter.

Hadley silently thanked the woman. They took the opportunity while Tyler's back was turned to step into line once more. After what Hadley said, he didn't stop to talk as he walked out the front door.

Relief blossomed into a great sigh once he was gone.

Suze whistled. "Luke and Tyler fighting over you. Crazy, huh?"

Hadley's mouth twisted into a frown. "They weren't fighting over me … they were just fighting, and I happened to be minimally attached to the subject matter that started said fight."

Her best friend shook her head as they stepped up to order. "Whatever you want to tell yourself, Had."

Suze's words lodged themselves into Hadley's chest,

making each breath tight and uncomfortable. Was she losing her touch? Suze hadn't come clean about sneaking around with Paul, after all. And Leo seemed like the most likely suspect despite her feelings otherwise.

Maybe she didn't know anyone as well as she thought she did anymore.

Being around all of the boxes at her house was beginning to stress Hadley out—especially since she still hadn't heard back from Deborah about her offer, and she couldn't stop thinking about the huge secret her so-called best friends were keeping from her—so she decided to spend a day in the jam kitchen. She shut her brain off and worked from muscle memory, making some more of her peach chutney. If she'd just run out of her supply from last summer, other people were bound to as well.

Her soul felt on the mend by the time she took the Jam Van to the post office to drop off some online orders for shipping. The sky was blue and cloudless. Maybe she would even get some gardening done after dinner.

Driving past the pharmacy, however, Hadley remembered she had just finished off her last bottle of sunscreen. She pulled over and headed inside to pick up some more. Her mother had always stressed the use of the stuff after Uncle Harold had a few patches of skin cancer removed.

The crisp, conditioned air of the pharmacy spilled out at Hadley as she pulled open the glass front door. She knew just where to go for the sunscreen, so she made a beeline for the aisle, knowing she was easily distracted by all of the other beauty products and trinkets they carried up front.

Her fingers brushed along the plastic containers of sunscreen until she found her favorite brand.

"Why do I need two?" Nadine, a mother of four was asking Hazel Smith at the prescription window. "This is just a precaution, right? I'm not going to have to stick this in Michael's leg, am I?"

It wasn't as if Hadley was one to listen in, especially not around people's medications, but Nadine and Hazel were both speaking just below a yell.

"Oh, totally a precaution, dear. More EpiPens get tossed because they've run through their expiration date than they do for being used. But they do recommend you carry two or more with you; put one in your purse and one in the house. That way you're prepared wherever, especially with a nut allergy like Michael's got. It's more likely he'll be triggered outside your home than inside." Hazel patted Nadine's hand. "And when school starts up again, you'll want to leave one there too."

Hadley remembered hearing about Nadine's youngest having a scare at school when he shared a peanut butter sandwich with a classmate and couldn't breathe afterward. They must've found out he was allergic.

Just as Hadley pointed herself toward the front of the store to pay, Hazel called out, "Why, if it isn't Stoneybrook's own Helen of Troy. Men fighting in the streets over that pretty face."

Cheeks burning with embarrassment, Hadley cringed and turned toward Hazel to set her straight. "Actually," she said with a forced smile, "it was about real estate, not me.

And I'd appreciate if you'd spread that as quickly as you can."

Hazel propped a hand on one hip. Even Nadine gave Hadley a pointed glare soaked in skepticism.

"If that's what two men look like fighting over a house, I'd hate to see what they might do to each other over a woman," Hazel said.

Hadley blushed and hustled up to the pharmacy register to purchase her sunscreen there instead of up front. But as she stepped outside into the summer sunshine, her embarrassment had turned to frustration. She'd been skipping through life thinking she knew people so well, thinking she knew what to expect from people she'd known her whole life. The last few days had proved how wrong she was to think that.

And if she couldn't even trust Suze and Paul, who was to say Leo wasn't also lying?

Hopping into the Jam Van, Hadley drove to Valley Wildflowers, fueled by anger and disappointment. For the first time since Charlie's death, Leo stood behind the counter instead of Jessie when she entered the shop.

Hadley gritted her teeth, working to hold on to the courage she'd found in her anger.

"Good afternoon, Miss James." Leo's kind face scrunched into a grin.

Hadley pushed her shoulders back and walked forward.

"I hear you're interested in the rental property," Leo added in her silence.

"I am." She stopped, softening for a moment before catching herself. "I know you're going to have many offers on the place, though, so I'm trying not to get my hopes up."

"That house holds so many happy memories for me." He smiled, his eyes reflecting his nostalgia. "I'd rather see it go to someone who's going to love it just as much as I did than make a mint off it. Though your Tyler might argue that I should answer that differently."

Hadley swallowed the uncomfortable lump which formed in her throat hearing him call Tyler hers. Back when they were in high school, the townspeople often referred to him as *your Tyler* or *that Henley boy of yours.* As they grew up and got married, it became *that husband of yours* along with many other variations. It was an odd sense of deja vu to hear him called as such again.

Catching sight of her expression, Leo tsked. "Oh dear. I'm so sorry, Hadley. Of course he's not yours anymore. The past few weeks have my mind all in a jumble. Seeing him back here again just brought back old memories of the two of you together, is all." His light-blue eyes caught hers.

"Yeah," Hadley said. "You're not the only one." She groaned.

"Ah. I've heard there was a bit of drama this morning."

She chuckled. "A bit? They're acting like teenagers. Worse, actually. I'm pretty sure Jessie hasn't ever done something so irrational and immature."

"Oh, I don't know." He shook his head. "She has her days."

"She's still young. Give her time. Heck, I got married at nineteen." Hadley shook her head. "I mean, Jessie's not doing anything *that* impulsive."

Leo clutched at his heart playfully, feigning a heart attack. "That would give me a fair shock, I have to admit. Though, she does have a new boyfriend I have yet to meet."

"Oh?" Hadley raised an eyebrow. She hadn't heard a thing about Jessie dating anyone. Normally that kind of news was front and center in the gossip rotation.

Smiling in that way fathers only can when getting to talk

about their kids, Leo added, "Told me they're getting serious, and she wants me to have dinner with him next week. I suppose this is what it's like watching your kids grow up, though. They stop needing you so much."

"Yeah, Deborah said she was staying at the rental property while she's home."

Leo waved a hand at Hadley. "Oh, it's not what Deborah thinks. I ripped out the flooring in her room a few months ago when we had a bit of a flooding problem with the laundry machine, but I'm not the handiest around, and I haven't gotten around to replacing it yet. It was either she stay out there or she crash on my couch all summer." He shrugged.

The lightness Hadley felt at hearing Leo talk about his daughter quickly dissipated when she caught sight of the half-empty jar of honey sitting on the counter top behind Leo. Charlie flirting with Jessie after threatening Leo's livelihood could've sent the normally rational man over the edge. It was all here. The honey behind him, the bees on his property, and his inability to provide an alibi.

Here she was, quite possibly standing alone with a murderer who knew her brother was closing in. What had she done? Blindly trusted someone, yet again, that's what. She needed to get out of there, and fast.

Leo must've noticed the way her expression had hardened. He followed her gaze behind him to the honey.

Trying to cover up why she'd been so interested, she asked, "Is that from the rental property? I noticed the beehive you had on the property when I was there."

Laughing, Leo shook his head. "Jessie got those bees for a project in middle school. We've never been brave enough to harvest any of the honey. Heck, I'm not even sure there are any still in there. This is Barry's honey. Jessie's been taking it to try to help with her allergies. Got me hooked on it too, in fact."

Hadley nodded and began backing away. Coming here alone had been a terrible idea. Nice as Leo seemed, every bit of evidence still pointed toward him. Thoughts scrambling, she came up with a lie.

"Well, it was actually Jessie I was hoping to talk to, but since she's not here …" She took one more step back.

"You might have more luck finding her than me, honestly." He sighed. "She's not answering my calls. I can't seem to find any of the supplies she picked up at the wholesale warehouse on her last trip." He opened a drawer and then closed it, the slam seeming to vent most of his frustration. "Sorry." His shoulders slumped forward. "I'm completely out of my normal wire card holders, and all I can find is this darn plastic one." He faked a shiver.

Hadley couldn't speak. But instead of her words being tangled in fear, they were wholly consumed with fitting together what Leo had just told her. No supplies? Had Paul or the other deputies even checked Jessie's warehouse alibi?

Her throat tightened further. What if it hadn't been Leo standing up to Charlie for the way he treated his daughter, but the daughter standing up for herself?

"Thanks, Leo. I'll see you around." Hadley croaked the words out before turning on her heel and heading outside. Her phone was in her grasp even before she hit the sidewalk. "Paul," she said when he answered on the first ring. "Did you guys get confirmation about Jessie being at that floral supply shop on the morning of Charlie's murder?"

He was silent for a moment. "From Stuart."

"Call right now and find out if they have a record of her coming in between eight and ten that morning," Hadley said, hoping they had security cameras.

❧ 24 ❧

Hadley paced back and forth in the jam kitchen, tapping her fingernails on the stainless-steel worktables as she passed by each time.

She stared at her phone sitting on the edge of one of the tables and willed Paul to call.

Come on. Please let there be a record of her there. Please let it just be a case of misplaced supplies.

A bell sound made her jump. But it wasn't the electronic ding of a text message or phone call. It was the jangling of the silver bells she kept on the back kitchen door. Looking behind her, Hadley suppressed a groan.

Luke walked into the kitchen.

Unlike Tyler, his face was unharmed, but her gaze flitted down to his fists, both slightly red—turning a bit blue—the left one sporting a nasty cut along the knuckles. So Tyler had been telling the truth—the man really *had* attacked him.

Hadley sighed. "Luke, I don't have—"

He put a bruised hand up. "Hazel Smith just called me and berated me for ten minutes about the nerve I had to jeopardize Tyler's pretty face when he was only standing up

185

for you. I came over right away to set things straight, because if that's the story Hazel has, it's the story everyone has."

"Story?" Hadley cocked an eyebrow, deciding to ignore how Hazel had definitely *not* followed her order to change the story she was telling folks.

"That's not what happened. At all." Luke's blue eyes held hers. They were the crisp, bright color of a perfect, cloudless, summer sky. He cleared his throat.

Hadley swallowed. She owed it to him to hear him out. After all, she had felt there was something off about Tyler's story. "So what happened?"

He rubbed the back of his neck and pushed back his shoulders. "He was running his mouth, and I socked him." Luke shrugged.

Hadley dropped her head to one side. "Oh, thank you for that detailed description. I feel so much better trusting you now."

She could see the muscles in his jaw clench together tight. He must've been gritting his teeth.

"Had, he was talking about you."

Blinking, she waited, signaling she needed more. When he didn't offer it up, she replied, "Okay … the man *is* allowed to talk about me without being assaulted."

He stiffened. "Not the stuff he was saying." Luke's eyebrows furrowed.

"What was he saying?" The question was smaller than she wanted it to come out, but her heart was beating too quickly, too loudly for anything stronger to come out.

Luke shook his head. "I don't want to repeat it."

Hadley reached out and grabbed Luke's arm. "I can handle it."

The man swallowed again. "I asked if you were getting

back together after seeing you two at the house the other day. He was adamant that you weren't, but said that he didn't cheat on you because you were bad in bed." Luke paused, discomfort twisting his features. "And he knew he'd be able to *get you in the sack* one last time, especially seeing how sentimental you were about selling the house."

Hadley's chest tightened. "So you punched him," she said, not a question this time.

"Not my best moment, but yeah." Luke hung his head, looking down at his bruised knuckles.

"So he didn't tell you to back off from Leo's place?"

"No. I hadn't even put in an offer. I called Deborah this morning before I even talked to Tyler to tell her I was out. I'm going to go with new construction on the other side of the lot from the tenant house."

Hadley blinked. "Well, that's news to me, Luke." She swatted at him. "I've been sitting here scared to death that you were going to blow me out of the water with your offer. You could've communicated a little better, you know."

He nodded. "I could've communicated a lot better. I'm not sure what came over me that day, why I felt the need to compete with you. I stopped by to tell you I wasn't going to fight you for it, but you were busy."

There was no time for her to respond because the door jingled again as Jessie walked into the kitchen.

"Hey," she said, beaming a bright smile in their direction. "Dad said you were looking for me." She noticed Luke and waved, her smile brightening even more at the sight of the handsome man.

Hadley could just about feel the adrenaline pulsing through her veins. Should she and Luke run? The girl didn't seem like a killer. She appeared as sweet and innocent as always.

"Um … yeah. I was looking for …" She stalled as she thought through something, anything to say which might make sense.

Hadley's phone rang out from the table behind her, saving her. "Hold on just one second," she said, jumping to retrieve her phone.

It was Paul. Finally. In her excitement, she swiped to answer the call. Her gaze flicked up to Jessie, then to Luke who was watching her. In that moment, she realized this was not the time nor the audience with which to answer this call.

She tried to hang up, but in her nervous fumbling it felt as if her fingers would only mash against the screen as the phone almost slipped from her grip.

"Hey, Paul. Hold on," she yelled at the screen, hoping she could cut him off, tell him it wasn't a good time.

But her clumsy screen mashing must've somehow engaged the speakerphone function, because when Paul's voice came through, it was loud enough to echo through the kitchen.

"We've checked the cameras and the transaction history for the only floral warehouse within three hours of here. There's no record of Jessie or Stuart," Paul said quickly, before she could hit the button again.

Her neck and face felt on fire as she turned slowly to look at Jessie and Luke. Jessie's eyes were wild and her body tensed. But in that moment Hadley's mind focused on someone other than Jessie.

Stuart! She'd forgotten about Stuart. If Jessie's alibi was false, so was Charlie's assistant manager's.

"I think it's gotta be Stuart, Had. I just can't figure out why Jessie would've lied for him." Paul continued to talk, unaware of the problem on the other end of the line.

Hadley's finger hovered over the speaker-phone button,

but it didn't seem necessary anymore. Jessie had heard everything. The girl's face turned pale, scared. That didn't seem to be the correct reaction for someone who claimed to hate Stuart.

Unless …

Stuart had mentioned he had a girlfriend, one who was constantly making him hold her belongings because her purse was too small. Hadley glanced at the tiny, just-bigger-than-a-phone bag that Jessie wore across her body, the small bag landing just at her hip.

Understanding came crashing down on Hadley like a whole box of jam jars falling off the shelf, startling and disturbing. Hadley's mind tried to organize the mess. Stuart hated Charlie for the way he'd treated him as a worker, knew everything about the man, had access to the van and his medication, and would've cared—a lot—when Charlie hit on Jessie.

"Had? You there?" Paul's voice crackled through the speaker.

"Because she's dating him. And together, they killed Charlie Lloyd." Hadley's voice shook as her mind flashed back to the drawer Stuart had shown her. There had been two pens in one place there. Stuart had said Charlie had the things spread out. Why double up two in one spot?

Because Stuart had been the one to move it from the van.

And the pink lipstick under the Bloom van must've been Jessie's.

Before Hadley could blink, Jessie's sneakers squeaked on the linoleum of the kitchen. She took off, slamming the door behind her. Luke followed a split second later.

"Paul, get McKay on the phone and tell him to arrest Stuart. Luke and I are in pursuit of Jessie." Hadley threw her phone onto the counter as she chased after them into the alley.

The screeching of tires and the heart-wrenching sound of someone screaming echoed off the brick buildings as Hadley ran down the alley and out onto Main Street.

Her eyes couldn't seem to take everything in at once when she emerged. People ran into the street. Tyler's shiny, black sedan was stopped in the middle of the road. Black rubber marking the concrete in lines a few feet behind the car.

And then there was Luke, clutching someone to his chest in the middle of it all.

"Give her space!" Luke commanded, holding out one hand as the other held Jessie tight.

Hadley ran in their direction. Jessie was standing— Hadley sent a thank you up into the heavens—and had her face buried in Luke's chest. She was sobbing, hitting him with one arm as she held the other one close to her body; it was scraped up, bleeding something fierce. Her jeans seemed to have saved her leg from similar road rash.

Tyler climbed out of the car and rubbed the back of his neck, obviously dumbstruck.

"She—she came out of nowhere!" He looked around as if hoping others would agree.

Hadley had no doubt she had with the hurry she'd been in to escape. She just hoped the girl hadn't broken any bones in the impact, with the car or the street.

The crowd parted as sirens blared from down the block by the town hall building. Paul's truck pulled up seconds later. He jumped out and ran over to Luke and Jessie. Hadley noticed the pair of handcuffs his hand rested on as he approached the two, but by the way Jessie looked up at him, tears and mascara staining her face, it didn't appear he would need them.

Especially when Leo ran out from the flower shop, having noticed the commotion. Jessie broke down into a whole new set of sobs.

Luke stood next to Hadley as Dr. Hall arrived on the scene to check out Jessie. Her father stood, talking to Paul, shaking his head the whole time, hand covering his mouth.

Hadley, overwhelmed by—well, everything—sank down to sit on the curb. She couldn't bear to watch as the paramedics finished their bandages, and Paul led Jessie to his truck. Luke sat next to her. The two of them were silent for a few moments. And while he didn't seem to know what to say any better than her, Luke's presence next to her did make her feel better.

She glanced up just in time to see Tyler narrow his gaze in their direction, or maybe the narrowing was more about the swelling in his bruised eye. Regardless, Hadley looked back down at her hands. Then she leaned into Luke until they were sitting shoulder to shoulder, like they used to when they were younger.

❧ 25 ❧

ONE WEEK LATER ...

Hadley opened the doors to Ansel and Marmalade's cat carriers. The difference between the two was almost laughable. Ansel, poked a pink nose out first, followed by a white-tipped paw. But Marmalade bounded out, racing in a circle around her bigger buddy, ready to play.

"Well, what do you two think of your new home?" she asked, smiling as she took in the mountain views and the sound of the rushing river.

The cats sniffed and walked the perimeter of the room in response. While she wasn't technically the owner of the house yet, Leo had let Hadley rent the place for the month until her closing date.

The sound of shoes scuffing on the wood floor behind her made Hadley turn to see Paul and Suze carrying in Hadley's queen-sized mattress, making it look almost effortless.

"You two make a pretty good team." She nodded in

approval, watching the two of them for any sign of discomfort, remorse, or even deceit. They simply smiled and disappeared into the master bedroom with the mattress.

Hadley had tried to create similar situations over the past few days, where it would be natural for them to come clean about their relationship, finally let her in on their secret. But they hadn't taken advantage of any of them.

At yet another failed attempt, Hadley's spirits sank. Since her discovery of Suze's hair stick in Paul's truck, Hadley had only become more convinced that they were hiding a relationship. What she wasn't able to figure out was why they were keeping it from her.

But today was moving day; she needed to focus on getting the last of her stuff moved into the house.

With one more glance back at the cats to make sure they were fine, she headed out to the moving van to help grab another box, feeling guilty for standing there when her family and friends were doing all of the heavy lifting.

She smiled as she passed by the small desk she had positioned at the front door for her purse and keys. A vase of sweet peas sat there with a congratulatory note from her parents saying they were sad to miss helping her move into her new home, but they would be home soon.

The moving van creaked and swayed as she approached. Hadley scaled the ramp and stopped herself as she almost ran smack into Luke, who was pulling out the largest piece of the bed frame and headboard her father had made for her.

"Whoops. Sorry." She sidestepped to get out of his way.

Luke winked at her before exiting down the ramp. The man had been in an exceptionally good mood, smiling, laughing, and even whistling. Hadley guessed it probably had to do with the fact that Tyler had left for Seattle a few days earlier.

Even though many eyewitnesses had concurred that Jessie had jumped in front of Tyler's car and he'd done everything he could to stop, she knew Tyler still felt guilty. He'd barely spoken to her when he'd pulled his rental truck up to the old house and loaded his belongings. And he hadn't brought up his fight with Luke again.

Hadley spotted two lamps near the front of the truck and wriggled them free. She began to whistle too.

🐝

Hours later, Paul closed the door to the rental truck with a clang. Luke thumped the metal bumper twice.

"That's a wrap," Paul said.

"Remind me to use you three when I'm moving my stuff into the new house, whenever it's finished, that is." Luke swiped sweat off his forehead with the back of his hand.

"Yeah, when's that going to be?" Suze asked.

"Considering I've still yet to decide on a design, a while. But this better be one rain check that doesn't expire."

They laughed and promised it wouldn't.

Paul checked his phone and frowned. "I've got to head down to the station. McKay's got Jessie and Stuart's court date set, and he wants me to go over the charges."

"He still only going to charge Jessie as an accessory?" Luke asked.

Paul said, "As far as I know. As of right now, she just provided Stuart with the bees and his alibi. He's the one who put the weapon in the van and hid the man's medication."

According to Stuart, Jessie hadn't been at the scene at

all. And while the lipstick had been hers, he claimed it must've fallen from his pocket, being one of the things she'd asked him to hold on to for her. Whether or not he was telling the truth or just protecting Jessie was something they hoped would become clear during the court proceedings.

The four of them shook their head. "Hotheaded teenagers," Suze said, her face etched with regret.

Paul wrapped an arm around her shoulder. "Watch it, old lady. You're starting to sound crochety."

Suze wrinkled her nose. "I'm three months older than you two." She pointed to Luke. "He's the old man."

Luke put his hands up in defense. "I'm sorry I was such a hyper kid that my mother didn't want to risk putting me in school too early. And that I'm lucky enough to be blessed with a summer birthday."

Suze made a gagging noise. "Get over yourself, Fenton. We already remembered that today's your birthday."

He laughed, but the smile was quickly replaced by a deadpan expression. "You did? I thought …"

Suze and Paul turned to glare at Hadley.

"Didn't you tell him?" Paul asked.

Hadley's cheeks heated up as she remembered. "Oh, right. Whoops." She cringed. "It's been crazy in my brain lately. I forgot."

Luke blinked, still lost. "Forgot what?"

"We're going to Seven Stones to celebrate later," Paul said. "I'll see you guys there after I meet with McKay."

"I'm going to hitch a ride into town with PJ," Suzanne said to Hadley, elbowing Paul playfully.

It was a gesture Hadley would never have thought twice about before, but this whole secrecy business was making her paranoid.

Suze seemed to catch Hadley's inquisitive glare because

she added, "I want to check on Leo. He's been hanging out at the sheriff's office more than he's been at home lately."

Paul nodded. "Poor guy. He could use the support."

Hadley chewed on her bottom lip as they waved and walked away, sure Leo had been getting more support from the town than he could ever imagine.

Luke leaned in as Paul's truck pulled away, leaving them alone. "Last time I saw him, the man was balancing three casseroles from the quilting society."

Maybe she was feeling particularly emotional because of the move. Or maybe it had to do with feeling like the third wheel all week since she'd figured out Paul and Suze's secret. But hearing Luke call out Suze's odd behavior made her want to hug him.

"Right?" she said, turning to face him. "Something's up with those two." She pressed her lips into a thin line.

"Oh, for sure." He nodded. "I don't think they could be anymore obvious about it, honestly."

Hadley blinked up at him. Had Luke figured it out too?

He opened his palms. "They're going to get me a surprise birthday present."

The laugh that spilled out of her served to vent most of her pent-up frustration. Luke smiled, obviously pleased with himself for getting such a reaction out of her.

He took a step back toward his own truck. "Well, I'll let you finish up here, then. You probably need time to wrap my present."

Hadley shook her head as she chuckled and waved goodbye to Luke. He was right, actually. She hadn't wrapped it yet. But she still wasn't sure how to wrap the new baseball cap she'd bought him to replace the dirty, red one. Maybe she could put it in a gift bag, instead. Snapping her fingers, she headed back inside.

"Now I just have to find where we put the box with my gift bags in it." She bit her lip as she thought.

A warmth spread through her as she closed the door and walking into the living room. Sunlight from the beautiful sunset streamed in through the huge picture windows covering the A-frame house.

Ansel and Marmalade were curled up together in the overstuffed chair she'd haphazardly shoved against the sliding glass door to make room for the couch.

"Home sweet home," she said out loud, letting the words reverberate through her chest.

Both of the following recipes are created by Marisa McClellan, creator of Food in Jars.

Honey-Sweetened Peach Chutney
Makes 8 half pints

4 pounds ripe yellow peaches (about 8-9 cups once peeled and chopped)

1 medium yellow onion, minced (about 1 cup)

2 cups golden raisins
1 3/4 cups red wine vinegar
1 1/2 cups honey
1 tablespoon mustard seeds (any color is fine)
1 tablespoon grated ginger
1 1/2 teaspoons sea salt
1/2 teaspoon red chili flakes
zest and juice of 1 lemon

Cut peaches into quarters and remove pits. Pile peaches into a large, heat-proof bowl.

Bring a kettle of water to a boil. Once it boils, pour the water over the peach quarters. Let them sit for 2-3 minutes, until the skins wrinkle and pull away from the fruit. Peel the skins away and chop the peaches.

In a large, non-reactive pot, combine the peaches, onion, raisins, vinegar, honey, mustard seeds, ginger, salt, red chili flakes, and lemon zest and juice.

Bring to a boil over high heat and then reduce the heat to medium-high. Cook, stirring regularly, at a brisk simmer for 45 minutes to an hour, until the chutney thickens, darkens, and the flavors start to marry.

While the chutney cooks, prepare a boiling water bath canner and sufficient jars.

When the chutney is finished cooking, funnel it into prepared jars, leaving 1/2 inch headspace. Wipe rims, apply lids and rings, and process in a boiling water bath canner for 15 minutes.

When time is up, remove jars from canner and place them on a folded kitchen towel to cool.

Once jars are cool enough to handle, remove rings and test seals. Sealed jars can be stored on the pantry shelf for up to a year. Unsealed jars should be refrigerated and used promptly.

※

Peach Lavender Jam
Makes 7 half pints

4 pounds ripe yellow peaches (about 8-9 cups once peeled and chopped)
    4 cups of sugar
    4 tablespoons powdered pectin
    1 lemon, juiced
    1 tablespoon dried lavender buds (make sure you're using culinary grade lavender)

Cut peaches into quarters and remove pits. Pile peaches into a large, heat-proof bowl.
    Bring a kettle of water to a boil. Once it boils, pour the water over the peach quarters. Let them sit for 2-3 minutes, until the skins wrinkle and pull away from the fruit. Peel the skins away and chop the peaches.

Prepare a boiling water bath canner and sufficient jars.

Place the chopped peaches in a large, non-reactive pot. Measure out the necessary sugar and whisk the pectin powder in to combine. Add the pectin-spiked sugar to the fruit and stir to incorporate. Add the lemon juice and stir again.

Place the lavender buds into a stainless steel tea ball or bundle them up in a length of cheesecloth (tie it tightly so that the lavender doesn't escape). Tuck the lavender packet into the pot with the fruit.

Once the sugar has started to dissolve and the peaches look very juicy, put the pot on the stove over high heat. Bring the fruit to a boil and reduce the heat to medium high. Let the jam bubble vigorously for 20-25 minutes, stirring regularly.

As the fruit cooks down, use a potato masher to break up the bigger peach pieces. This gives a better texture and will prevent fruit and jelly separation later on.

The jam is finished when it has reduced in volume by at least one-third, is visibly thicker, and looks quite glossy.

Turn off the heat under the jam, remove the lavender packet, and stir the jam for a few moments off the heat. Funnel the jam into the prepared jars, leaving 1/2 inch headspace. Wipe the rims, apply the lids and rings, and process in a boiling water bath canner for 10 minutes.

When time is up, remove jars from canner and let cool on a folded kitchen towel. When jars are cool enough to handle, remove rings and test seals. Any unsealed jars should be refrigerated. All sealed jars are safe for shelf storage.

Visit Marisa's blog and website, Food in Jars, for tons of recipes, tips, product reviews, and links to her books.

DON'T MISS THE NEXT BOOK IN THE STONEYBROOK SERIES:

Follow Hadley, Paul, Suze, and Luke as they solve another mystery in the small town of Stoneybrook. Miranda, the sweet girl who works at the local candy shop, is missing after another teen is found dead in Cascade Ridge. Can they find her before she becomes another victim?

PRE-ORDER YOUR COPY TODAY!

ABOUT THE AUTHOR

Eryn Scott lives in the Pacific Northwest with her husband and their quirky animals. She loves classic literature, musicals, knitting, and hiking. She writes cozy mysteries and women's fiction.

Join her mailing list to learn about new releases and sales!

www.erynwrites.com
erynwrites@gmail.com

ALSO BY ERYN SCOTT

MYSTERY:

The Pepper Brooks Cozy Mystery Series

The Stoneybrook Mysteries

WOMEN'S FICTION:

The Beauty of Perhaps

Settling Up

The What's in a Name Series

In Her Way

ROMANTIC COMEDY:

Meet Me in the Middle

Made in the USA
Middletown, DE
03 July 2019